Her scalp tingled in sudden fear....

She turned cautiously. Someone was definitely watching her, concealed in the teeming marketplace of old Damascus.

Then she spotted Tony Belmont—the man who was blackmailing her. The blood drained from her face; she willed her legs to run, but it was useless— this time he had her cornered. Terrified, she met the flat, malevolent gaze of her assailant. He gave her an ugly smile.

"I'm just here to collect what's coming to me. I won't be too rough with you, Eleanor...not yet."

Other

MYSTIQUE BOOKS

by LILIANE ROBIN

The Snare

by LILLIANE ROBIN

MYSTIQUE BOOKS

TORONTO•LONDON•NEW YORK
HAMBURG•AMSTERDAM•STOCKHOLM

THE SNARE / first published September 1980

ISBN 0-373-50096-3

PRINTED IN U.S.A.

Chapter 1

The hectic Paris traffic hissed along the rue Passy, splashing April puddles onto the dismal sidewalks. Eleanor frowned as she leaped back out of the path of the pelting spray and said something impolite under her breath. She wondered if she'd ever get across the street. She could see the sign, glowing wetly—a beacon in the rainy night: Hotel Ariana.

She'd found it at last. All that stood between her and her goal was this never ending river of small French automobiles, speeding through the rain with headlights blazing, each driver determined to outrace the next, snapping in and out of lanes— and all of them absolutely heedless of her.

Grimly Eleanor looked up and down the street. Leave it to Derek to find a hotel in this off-the-track district, she thought. There didn't seem to be traffic lights anywhere. The small suitcase dragged heavily on her arm. . . .

Eleanor sighed, hoisting her umbrella a little higher, and resigned herself to waiting for a gap in the traffic. It would be suicide to step out now, even though she knew steel-nerved Parisians did it all the time.

She waited under the scented, dripping chestnut trees, measuring her chances and mentally listing the things she would say to her stepbrother Derek when she'd caught up to him at last.

But here was her chance—a Citroën swept by, and after it, surely for a hundred yards, there was nothing. It was now or never!

Eleanor boldly ran across the first lane of the boulevard, hoping her not-so-sensible shoes wouldn't betray her, and gasped as she saw headlights bearing down with alarming speed. Quickly she turned her head to the right. The cars coming the other way—were they far enough off?

Horns blared. There was no time to think. Blindly she dashed across to the far sidewalk, gaining safety by a whisker as the aggressive Gallic drivers honked and swore.

She stood for a moment with her heart pounding and thanked whatever stars had preserved her on this very last leg of her journey. She'd come all the way from Victoria, British Columbia, on boats and buses, in planes, taxis and subways. It had taken her twenty straight hours, and she had slept for very few of those.

And at last here was the Hotel Ariana, small but comfortably old.

The tiredness and annoyance seemed to drain

from her. She looked up at the sign; it was neon, yet discreet. She fervently hoped the place was respectable, then smiled to herself at the thought of finally seeing Derek.

She walked confidently up the steps of the hotel. The headlights of the rushing cars behind her were reflected in the cheerful polished brass of the door and twinkled in the grooves of its beveled glass. Within, yellow lamps glowed in the lobby. Gratefully Eleanor pulled the door open and stepped inside.

The clerk stared at her. For a moment she was sure her hesitant French had confused the man. She tried again. "Darnay...Derek Darnay. Do you have anyone registered here by that name?" She smiled uncertainly.

"Ah, mademoiselle...we do not. I am sorry... no one by that name...." The clerk peered at her through thick eyeglasses. His face was closed, suspicious.

Eleanor was dismayed. No Derek? Not after all this. Surely this was the right hotel: Ariana, rue Passy.... Even now she could hear Derek's voice over the telephone: "The Ariana—I'll meet you there."

Three days ago the telephone had seemed like her only connection with reality—a long, slender cord, which magically connected the continents, crossed seas and prairies and cities to link her with Derek. And now that thin, bright thread had snapped. She was alone.

She brushed the hair from her forehead, feeling

awkward. The brief happiness that had filled her as she entered the old-fashioned elegance of the Ariana's lobby was abruptly gone now, leaving behind a sense of bleakness and confusion.

The clerk continued to stare at her, his pale eyes solemn behind the flat, reflecting lenses of his spectacles.

"You're... perfectly certain?" she stammered, unsure of the proper French phrase.

The young man looked annoyed. "I am indeed perfectly sure," he answered in smoothly accented English. "In fact, in the last twenty-four hours you are the third person to inquire about this man. And for the third time I must say we have no reservation, no information."

Eleanor felt a sense of foreboding steal over her. People had been asking for Derek. But who, she wondered. She must have allowed her alarm to show on her face, for the clerk suddenly leaned closer.

"In fact, I don't mind telling you that I have every reason to believe that one of those interested inquiries came from the police," he said, emphasizing this piece of information with mock disdain.

"The police?" Eleanor's stomach wrenched. Derek and the police. It wasn't an unfamiliar link. Derek had been getting into trouble for years, but she'd never got used to it. She had an urge to leave the hotel quickly now, to escape the cold stare of this stranger and the old anger she felt at her stepbrother's irresponsible behavior.

But that made no sense at all. She had not come

this long, long way *not* to see him. And see him she would, Eleanor decided. Right now she was terribly tired, and there seemed only one thing to do. She stood very straight and looked the hotel clerk in the eye.

"I'm certain you're wrong about the police. Nevertheless, whether Monsieur Darnay is here or not, I would like a room for myself," she said authoritatively.

Caught off balance, the room clerk reverted to a polite and professional manner. "Certainly, *mademoiselle*. Without delay." He fumbled for a moment, placing the register in front of her.

"Do you have a single with bath?" Eleanor demanded.

"Yes, we have several. There's one on the seventh floor, for example, with a magnificent view of Paris."

"I'd rather have one farther down, on the third or fourth floor."

"The rooms on those floors are smaller, and of course, the view isn't as good."

"I don't mind that," she said crisply.

The clerk looked through his card file. "I have a room on the second floor and one on the third."

"I'll take the one on the third."

"Very well. May I ask how long you're planning to stay?"

"I don't know yet. It will depend on . . . various things."

The clerk nodded and handed her a printed registration form. "Please fill this out when you have time." He took a key from the board, signaled to a bellhop and ordered, "Take this lady to room forty."

The bellhop took Eleanor's small bag. After a short ride in an antiquated elevator, he led her into the room.

"Wait a minute, please," she said to him when he had put down the bag and was about to leave. She quickly filled out the registration form, indicating her name as Eleanor Hamilton and her nationality as Canadian. She handed it to the bellhop along with a tip.

As soon as he had gone, Eleanor went into the bathroom and splashed cold water on her face. The mirror above the basin reflected her drawn features. Her eyes glistened with restrained tears. She had been clinging still to her illusions when she came into the Hotel Ariana. Now they were gone.

Like an automaton, she stared at her mirror self. Appropriately enough, the dampness had made her ash blond curls limp; the normally sea-green eyes seemed dark and lifeless. There was a spatter of raindrops on the shoulders of her coat. Wearily she slipped it off.

Damn him. Damn Derek anyway! The words were childish, automatic. She had said them often enough before.

No wonder he couldn't come home when mother was ill. No wonder he "couldn't make it" to the funeral, she fumed. He was far too busy with whatever rotten little business he had in Paris.

Furious, she whirled and stalked from the bathroom to toss her coat onto the bed. She flopped down into a chair and kicked off her shoes. She tried to think. She was so tired, bone tired. Her hands shook as she rubbed her eyes, trying to will away the hot tears that were coming now, unstoppable, coursing down her cheeks.

How could he let her down *again*, she asked herself hopelessly. How could he *always* let her down? He'd been so warm, so reassuring on the telephone—a source of brotherly strength. He was the only "family" left now.

"I need to see you, to get away now," she'd said. "I'm so upset—mother's illness was hard."

"I know, I know." Derek's voice had been far away but familiar on the transatlantic phone. "Tell you what...I'm sort of between apartments and can't really put you up, but you come and we'll get you into a nice hotel. I'll make it up, Ellie. I know I didn't come. But I couldn't have helped— you know that...."

"She wanted to see you. You *never* came home, Derek."

"Please, Ellie...I couldn't. But come to Paris. Go to the Hotel Ariana. Seven hundred eighty-six rue Passy. I'll meet you there. Ask at the desk."

"Derek, I'm coming right away...."

That had been three days earlier. Now here she was, with no Derek to welcome her. And the police—they were looking for him. What was it this time? Drugs? Stolen goods?

Derek's "scrapes" had started a long time before. He'd already been a wild, unruly boy by the time Eleanor's mother had married his father. Eleanor was slightly older, but she and Derek had become very close in those school years in Victoria. She had tried hard to restrain him, to keep him away from the rough, bored boys who got their kicks any way they could in that staid little city.

It had been a losing struggle. Derek had been motherless for too long, and his father's bewildered, angry rantings had seemed to make matters worse.

By the time Eleanor was in university, Derek had been in and out of various kinds of trouble with the law many times: joyriding in stolen cars; hubcaps sold on an underground black market, drugs smoked, drugs "dropped"; visits by constables, square-shouldered and threatening, at strange hours of the night. . . .

Derek had not been sobered by his father's death five years ago. He had moved to Vancouver, a bigger city, with a bigger, more sinister underworld. He had played with fire, skirting the fringes of real crime and always managing to escape real punishment.

Once or twice he'd been given a suspended sentence, on the strength of his stepmother's solemn pleas that he'd behave in her care. He would come home, contrite, charming—always charming. And very sincere in his efforts to "straighten out." Eleanor and her mother tried to gain his trust and made promises to everyone they knew in order to get him jobs and help him stay away from the bad company he always seemed to keep.

Bad company. Like Tony Belmont.

Eleanor's mouth flooded with bitter distaste at the thought of the dark-haired young man who'd been the source of Derek's last real trouble in Victoria. He had been presentable enough on the surface. Perhaps he was a bit expensively dressed for the kind of job he held down at the auto-parts warehouse with Derek. But Tony was always polite and smooth-tongued, with a certain acquired sophistication.

At first Eleanor's mother had been impressed. "That boy's ambitious," she would say. "Not like those young hoodlums Derek knows. Perhaps he'll be a good influence."

Eleanor felt a twinge of sadness at the memory of her mother's naive trust. But Tony had been hard to judge. They had hoped so much that Derek would "come out of it," learn to work for what he wanted. . . .

When Tony began to ask Eleanor out, she'd been willing enough. It was a way to do normal everyday things, to go with Derek and his date to dinners at small restaurants, to the movies or the beach. Tony was older than Derek—the right age for Eleanor. It was little enough trouble to befriend him, to take time from her university studies and relax and keep an eye on Derek at the same time.

But it hadn't lasted.

Eleanor could not learn to like Tony, and when

he began to make sly, unwanted passes at her, she had been forced to stop seeing him. He became overbearing in an ugly manner, calling her in the middle of the night with insinuating propositions and sending vulgar notes and telegrams to the door. Eleanor had managed to hide his obnoxious behavior from her mother. She hoped that if she ignored him firmly enough, he would just give up.

But Tony's ego had no room for this rejection. He continued to harass Eleanor like a man obsessed until the sight of him began to sicken her. His unwelcome endearments degenerated into threats. Eleanor was at her wits' end, simply trying to stay away from him while he smilingly worked his way into her mother's confidence, becoming a fixture in the household.

Eleanor's problem had been solved in a dramatic, if jolting, fashion. One night the police appeared—detectives, this time in plain clothes, who demanded to know where Derek was. Eleanor and her mother were at a complete loss. It had happened again. And this time there was no way out.

Derek was arrested along with Tony for stealing large amounts of merchandise from the warehouse and shipping them to underworld connections in cities across the country. Tony had the connections, it turned out, and had been pilfering for years. At the trial a penitentiary term had seemed certain.

Derek's wayward angel had been on hand, however. He was acquitted on a technicality while Tony was sent to jail.

Derek had then announced his intention to get away, to see the world and start a new life. "I've been lucky," he said, "and now I'm going to make it all work out. You'll see!" He had gone to Europe and settled in Paris, writing glowing reports of his new horizons and his elaborate, if vague, plans for the future.

For nearly three years Eleanor and her mother had heard nothing but these buoyant reports. No crimes, no police, just Derek, becoming a man at last. Gradually Eleanor's fears had dulled. Surely she and her mother could believe now that Derek really was reshaping his life....

But tonight Eleanor knew with numbing certainty that the same old story was playing itself out. Derek and the police...it was an inevitable connection.

She sighed. Where was he now? She rose from the chair, physically shaking off the bitter burden of the past. It was time to go to bed...to try to sleep. Things would be clearer in the morning.

Wearily she began to undress. With dreamlike motions she hung the jacket of her gray traveling suit in the closet and with stiff fingers began to unbutton her blouse. The details of the room barely registered on her: the polished wood of the elegant little bed; the snowy pillows, softly inviting; the dresser top where she could lay out her cosmetics in the morning—or whenever she awoke. She was certain that she'd sleep forever, or at least for a day or two. Even now as she stood in the yellow lamplight, her eyelids were sagging.

Suddenly Eleanor's taut nerves tingled with alertness. There had been a small sound. Something quite out of place, the faintest squeak. She turned with animal precision to its source, the door.

As she watched with widening eyes, the handle slowly turned—tentatively, very softly.

Rooted to the spot, she stared at the knob. Her heart began to pound heavily. She tried to call out, but her throat was dry and constricted. No sound would come.

The lock! Had she locked it? Surely she had! But a mental image rocketed through her mind of the bellhop, going out—and of herself, walking straight into the bathroom. She hadn't locked the door! She knew it with crushing certainty. Here, alone in a strange hotel in a strange city, she had forgotten to lock the door. *Idiot*, she mentally chided.

Adrenalin flooded her body. She snatched up the blouse she'd just taken off and held it in front of her protectively. In almost the same motion she moved toward the door quickly and quietly. If she could just reach it, to snap on the lock....

But it was too late. The door knob moved decisively, and there was a loud clicking sound as the catch shifted. The door began to open.

Eleanor's breath caught painfully in her throat. Instinctively she backed away, catlike in her stockinged feet. She looked desperately around for some kind of escape. The telephone! It sat, impassive, silent, on a table...ten feet away. If she could get to it, quickly call the desk—

She dove for the phone, still mindlessly clutching the blouse in front of her.

A sneering voice brought her up short. "Well, well! How convenient."

The voice was familiar. Too familiar. It tore at her strained nerves like a jagged saw. Eleanor spun around, an involuntary sob escaping from her throat.

The opaque, humorless eyes took her in with an air of triumph.

"You really should remember to lock your door, Eleanor," Tony Belmont whispered.

Chapter 2

Eleanor's head seemed to spin for a moment as she stared in disbelief. That grinning, arrogant face had to belong to somebody else, someone in a mask. But no, it definitely was Tony Belmont.

Revulsion welled in her. "What do you think you're doing? This is my room!"

"Just thought I'd drop in—it's not often I run into half-naked ladies, even in Paris," Tony said as his eyes slid over her.

Eleanor's pulse pounded with anger. "You can't just walk in like this!" She was horribly conscious of her half-dressed state.

"Come on, it's only me, Tony. Remember?"

"I remember far too well. What are you doing here?" demanded Eleanor.

"I'm sure you know perfectly well. And stop quaking like a butterfly. I've always been a gentleman, haven't I?"

Eleanor's anger brought a steely edge to her voice. "I'm not quaking. And you've never been a gentleman. Stop leering at me or I'll call downstairs." Eleanor began to step sideways into the bathroom.

"Calm down, lady. I haven't got time for romance," Tony sneered.

Moving quickly, Eleanor pulled the bathroom door shut and struggled into the blouse. The sight of Tony had brought a rush of ugly memories. She fought to control a tide of panic, remembering his insistent pawing, his obsessive attentions in the past.

He was probably the last person on earth she wanted to see. *Tony, here in Paris.* Quick connections leaped through her mind. Derek must be mixed up with him again. How else could he have known she was here?

Tony's voice came through the door, laced with elaborate sarcasm. "Come on out. I won't hurt you...."

Said the spider to the fly, Eleanor thought angrily. She brushed the pale curls off her face and gave herself a resolute stare in the mirror. Well, whatever he was doing here, he wouldn't stay long. She would make certain of that. Taking a deep breath, she stepped back into the room.

She stared hard at him. He hadn't changed at all. He was the same Tony—the same insinuating, leering Tony, dressed to kill and watching her with greedy eyes.

"All right," she said firmly. "What's going on?"

"Gee," said Tony, lolling now in the armchair, "That's what I was going to ask you."

"What do you mean by barging in here?" asked Eleanor, pointedly ignoring the direction of his gaze.

"I'm here on business," he replied lightly. "Though I've got to admit it's a pleasant surprise to run into you, Eleanor, and to see you looking so, er, charmingly disarranged."

"I don't know what you're talking about, Tony, but I'll give you exactly thirty seconds to explain."

Tony's face darkened abruptly, and he stood up.

"*You* explain, Eleanor, and do it quick. Where's Derek?"

"I don't know where he is," she replied coolly.

Eleanor's mind shot back to her confrontation with the hotel clerk. Three people had asked for Derek. Tony must have been one of them!

"Don't hand me that," Tony snarled, starting toward her. "You know damned well where he is, and you're going to tell me." His hand shot out, half-raised as if to strike her.

Eleanor stepped back, rigid. "Tony, don't *ever* try anything like that!" Her words were sharp and precise while her jaw clenched in anger.

Tony's face creased into an ugly grin. "Spitfire, huh? Always liked that in you, Eleanor." But he backed off, and sitting down again, assumed an air of affability.

"Look, you and I can cooperate on this. Why be greedy? I know he's given it to you. That's why you're here. Don't think I didn't watch the hotel.

Don't underestimate me. I couldn't figure out
what the hell he had in mind, but when my wandering eyes saw *you* cross the boulevard and trot
into the hotel, I knew. Clever, very clever."

Eleanor stared at him. "What's clever? And I
hope you don't think I'd get involved with any of
the garbage you two are mixed up in. . . ."

"Come *on*! I've got no time to waste! He
thought he'd do me out of this one, get away with
the whole bag by laying it on you. But he forgot—I know you, even if the cops don't."

Something seemed to snap inside Eleanor.
"Look, Tony, I don't have the faintest idea what
you're talking about. Derek isn't here, has not
been here—and if he tries to palm off anything at
all on me, anything *you* want, he'll have to think
about it twice. Because I'm *not* involved! Now,
why don't you just go away? If you don't, I'm going to make such a racket. . . ."

"All right, all right." Tony glowered at her. "I
can see I'm not going to get anywhere."

He stood up, looking suspiciously around the
room. Then he turned and spoke slowly, emphat-
ically jabbing a finger at her. "But I'm watching.
Remember that and don't forget to tell Derek. He's
not going to work *this* cross, not on Tony Belmont. We were partners, and if he thinks he can
pull a number, take the money and run—" Tony
grinned darkly "—well, not so, baby, not so. I'll
get him and I'll get you if it takes me forever."

Before Eleanor could stop him, Tony hooked an
arm around her neck and pulled her hard against
his chest. "Don't forget—I'm watching," he

breathed, his face unbearably close to hers. He grinned again and abruptly flung her away from him.

Stunned, Eleanor could not will herself to move or speak. Tony stepped silently through the door. As he was pulling it shut, he turned to her with a familiar leer. "Still love me?" he asked and smiled more broadly as Eleanor winced. He ducked out and slammed the door, but he wasn't gone. He opened the door again smoothly. His voice dropped to a whisper as he added, "And you really should remember to lock your door...."

Angrily Eleanor rushed toward him and gave the door a sharp, final push. With trembling fingers she locked it.

She stood for a long while, her back rigid against the door, waiting for the pounding in her head to stop. As her rapid breathing subsided, and her mind slowly cleansed itself of the image of Tony's face, the harsh sounds of his words, one clear thought emerged: she must get out of there the following day, go back to Canada. Whatever mess Derek was in this time had robbed her of her affection for him. She felt a deadness, a limp depression. There truly was no one, no one in the world.

She had been foolish to hope, to reach out to Derek, to imagine that he'd changed, that he'd be able to help her through the time of grief and loss.

Eleanor's exhaustion overtook her, and her legs trembled. There was nothing to do but get into bed now, to sleep at last.

GRAY POOLS OF LIGHT stole into the room, picking out shapes. Strange darknesses and shadowy hollows yielded to the morning and became doorways, tables, lamps.

Eleanor was suddenly wide-eyed. Where was she? This dim chamber—was it part of the chaos of her dreams?

The facts came to her one by one. She was in Paris. These pillows, kind and enfolding, belonged to a Paris hotel, the Ariana. Derek had not met her, but there had been Tony. He had leaned into her face and said ugly things. . . .

Eleanor sat up, shaking off the images of the previous night. What was she to do? And where was Derek? She knew she had dreamed of him and of the times when they had been close.

She looked at her watch and saw its second hand sweeping calmly around the dial. She tilted it toward the light: 6:10 A.M. Too early to do anything, and besides, she was too tired, she thought. *Why am I awake? Brain, just let me sleep a little while more.* Then she flopped back down onto the pillows, but it was no use. Her mind was a welter of jumbled voices, of shifting images: Tony, Derek, the long trip from the Canadian west coast to Paris, France.

Perhaps there was nothing to do but get up. She crept gingerly out of bed, testing her tired legs and shaking her head.

She went to the window and looked out. The street was gray and deserted. Shallow puddles were left over from the rain of the day before; they reflected a flat, neutral sky that promised little for the day.

So this is Paris, she thought wryly, echoing everybody's cliché. It looked bare and peaceful, cleared of traffic and people. Chimney pots made a crazy pattern in every direction. . . .

A walk, quiet and alone, in those bleak streets, she mused, with no one around to know she didn't belong here: that was the cure for her confusion. Eleanor imagined the feel of the cool spring air on her face. It would clear her head, and then perhaps she could think.

She ran a bath, trying to keep the taps quiet, and sorted out her clothes. A pair of tailored slacks, her really sensible shoes, a sweater. Sinking into the tub, she allowed the water to soak out the last of her weariness, and shampooed her hair with vigorous, massaging fingers.

A few brush strokes fluffed the naturally rebellious curls dry. She dressed and collected her key, taking some francs bought at Le Bourget Airport. Perhaps a café would be open for coffee and a croissant? Then she slipped out of her room into the silent, red-carpeted hallway.

STEPPING FROM THE DESERTED HOTEL lobby into the street, Eleanor found herself looking both ways carefully and scanning the opposite side of the rue Passy. Was Tony there, silently watching, as he had said he would be, she wondered. She could see no one.

She told herself to relax. Tony was nothing but a common punk. She wasn't afraid of him. And she wasn't going to let him and his threats prey upon her mind. How he'd like that, she thought, squaring her shoulders and walking briskly along the boulevard.

It was just 6:40; Paris still slept, although an occasional car passed by. Eleanor decided to escape even this small sign of human activity and turned to her left into a narrow, winding side street. The fact that she had no idea where the cobbled little thoroughfare might lead seemed to add immensely to its charm.

The gray-fronted houses crowded close to the narrow sidewalk, and trees, thick with the new leaves of spring, leaned here and there over wrought-iron fences.

Eleanor drank in the cool and fragrant air, the special air of Paris, heady with tree scent and moist with the previous night's rain.

She strolled slowly, taking in the details of the street and the narrow buildings, five or six stories tall, crowding one upon the other, with carved cornices and slate-shingled roofs and geraniums dotted in the windows. Sleepy carols came from the trees as sparrows celebrated the morning. A pleasant, tentative breeze riffled the leaves and puffed softly in Eleanor's hair.

She tried to orient herself. Where was she in relation to the hotel? The side street had jogged and turned several times, and she had crossed two or three quiet avenues...but she wasn't really lost. All she would have to do would be to return exactly the way she came.

She was pleased with herself. She had gotten

away from the oppressive sense that Tony was watching her. She was free of his threats.

She wondered again where Derek could be. Perhaps she should stay at the hotel after all, at least for a day or two. It would be foolish to check out now, to run back to Canada just because Tony had talked about some kind of sordid business between himself and Derek.

She smiled to herself. Derek would never learn, but he had never really hurt anyone with his excesses. Besides, she had only Tony's word for it that Derek was involved with anything illegal. She probably should wait and see. The old fondness, the urge to see him, had returned. She only hoped he would have the sense to call her soon.

Eleanor found that her little side street had led to a very ancient cul-de-sac. She stood at the center of a square where the buildings stood tall, blocking much of the light. In the deep shadows green moss crept up the walls, and there was a strange silence, an air of expectancy. Even the birds had stopped twittering. Eleanor had the impression that here, in this old quarter, nothing had changed much for many years—perhaps for centuries.

Suddenly she was alert, her ears attuned to a new sound in the silent morning. She heard footsteps, their sound at first indistinct, then growing louder. The steps moved along the pavement, coming closer. They echoed in the deserted street. Unhurried, they drew steadily closer to the little square.

Irrationally, there in the heightened reality of the morning, Eleanor was afraid. She felt trapped.

There was nowhere to go, only back toward the footsteps. But she did not want to go back that way, to come face to face with whoever was following her. She was frozen, rooted to the spot, while the staccato sound echoed louder and louder.

She thought of Tony. The footsteps must be his. He was watching her, following her as he had said he would. She felt her stomach tighten.

But a sensible inner voice came to her rescue. *Here you are in Paris, France*, it said firmly. *It is broad daylight. Stop acting like a rabbit caught in a trap. If Tony's following you, you can get away.*

She willed her own reluctant feet to escape from the dead-end street. Moving into the shelter of a brick wall, she looked cautiously toward the entrance to the square. She felt the rough texture of the mortar under her fingers as she inched her way along and smelled the rich green dampness of moss. Over this wall there must be an ordinary world where everyday Frenchmen drank their everyday coffee and got ready for their ordinary jobs....

And here she was, creeping along like some sort of spy, her heart a trip-hammer in her chest as she strained to see who was walking behind her, who had followed her into the little square.

He strode confidently into the court. She had made her way along the wall to a place where he could not see her without turning. Only his back was visible: the tall, rather slender form, the dark hair...it *was* Tony!

Her heart gave a heavy jerk. Unreasonably, she wanted to run. She knew she ought to challenge him, to demand that he leave her alone. But an instinctive, powerful voice spoke more strongly within her: *Run! Get away. Don't let him know he's trapped you here—don't give him the satisfaction....*

She moved silently. A few more steps took her around the corner of the wall, out of the square.

And then, crazily, she began to run. Propelled by the desire to be free of him, her body moved strongly, carrying her away from the little square and heedlessly through the maze of streets. She was strangely elated, almost flying. Poor Tony! Just let him try to catch her, to torment her! She looked over her shoulder several times. There was no sign of him.

At last she slowed to a walk, conscious now of a few other people in the streets, ordinary, safe people on their way to work. Her breathing was tumultuous, and she tried to calm it, taking in and releasing air in deliberate gulps.

She suppressed a smile, thinking she must look strange to these sophisticated Parisians. A glimpse in a shop window confirmed that she was looking more than a little casual—perhaps even windblown! It was time to get back to the hotel. But where *was* the hotel, Eleanor wondered.

In her rush to get away from Tony she had paid no attention whatever to the streets she'd passed. Now she was thoroughly lost!

Judging from the general direction from which

she had come, however, she was now several blocks to the west of the rue Passy. She checked a few street signs and calculated that if she took the broad avenue just ahead, she could approach the Hotel Ariana by a roundabout route, avoiding any retracing of the maze of back streets where she'd just narrowly missed Tony.

Eleanor walked confidently now, taking in the sights and sounds of the awakening city: the rushing cars, ever more numerous in the avenue; the jostling, noisy, aggressive groups of students, hurrying intently along, books under their arms; the career girls, walking briskly in clothes that were unmistakably Parisian. She passed several open-fronted cafés, saw people with croissants, café au lait and morning newspapers. Watery sunshine was reflected in the leftover rain puddles and glinted on shop windows.

Kiosks advertised the latest plays and concerts; gendarmes controlled the traffic. Eleanor busied herself reading signs and newspaper headlines, practicing her French. She had begun to enjoy herself. Perhaps she should sit for a while in a café.

The next café I see, the next really nice one, she thought, *I'll sit down.* The milky coffee would taste very good right now.

The street curved to Eleanor's right under a cluster of low, blooming chestnuts, and she almost bumped into him before his image registered: the shoulders, square in the tan raincoat, the one she'd seen in the cul-de-sac, the dark hair.... Tony again!

He was standing in front of her, his back turned. He gazed into a shop window.

Eleanor checked herself in time to avoid colliding with him. He could not have seen her—*must* not have seen her. To her dismay her heart began to thud again. The irrational feeling of fear had returned. He seemed to be everywhere!

She whirled quickly to retreat, to get away.

His voice cut throught the city noises and the pounding at her temples. "*Mademoiselle!*"

But that wasn't Tony's voice; it was a deeper voice, and the accent was unmistakably French. In spite of herself Eleanor turned.

Instead of Tony's flat, dark eyes she was met by an electric, sky-blue gaze. True, his hair was dark, but it was even darker than Tony's. And it fell over a high, chiseled forehead that resembled Tony's not at all.

Embarrassed, Eleanor turned away, anxious to escape.

"*Mademoiselle, un moment,*" said the man, his voice urgent. She felt a hand on her arm.

Eleanor faced him again. "I'm sorry," she said. "My French is poor.... *Je ne parle pas....*"

"Oh, but I speak English! Please, you must explain yourself." The blue eyes seemed to dance with amusement. "This is the second time this morning that I've turned around, only to see you scampering away from me."

Eleanor felt herself blush to the very roots of her curls.

"Come on," he pleaded. "Am I so bad? But

wait. I can see it. You are frightened a little. . . ." The mockery disappeared, and concern darkened the blue of his eyes.

"No. . . really I'm not. I just thought you were someone else, that's all. I'm fine." She smiled up at him, and he looked suddenly relieved.

"Thank goodness! I was having the most extraordinary fantasies about you—that you were some sort of spirit, sent to haunt the little square—"

Eleanor laughed. "I guess *I* was the one being spooked. You see, I heard your footsteps, and in that lonely place with no one around. . . I got carried away. . . ."

He folded his arms. "Well, I suppose that explains it. But you must let me buy you coffee, to make up for frightening you. I must know more of this story."

It would be easy to talk to this stranger, Eleanor sensed. And she needed a friend badly. But he was too handsome and charming—surely a man of the world. Friendship was probably not his intention, if he had one. Eleanor was wary of strangers right now.

"Thank you, but I'm in rather a hurry." She smiled her best smile and was gratified to see real disappointment in his eyes.

"I see," he said. Then he smiled back at her. His teeth were very white against the darkly tanned skin. He gave a little bow. "Well, then, perhaps we'll meet yet again, *mademoiselle.*"

"Perhaps," said Eleanor airily as she strolled

away. Probably not, she thought. Oh well, with
that tan he was more than likely an idle playboy
just back from the Mediterranean. Not her type at
all. . . .

A little regretfully she concentrated on the
business at hand. After consulting for directions
with a gendarme, she decided to get back to the
Hotel Ariana after all and to have her coffee there.

So Tony had not shadowed her movements this
morning! She felt light and free again. Perhaps
Derek had called, or was trying to get in touch
with her.

At the hotel desk she picked up her key and
learned there were no messages.

She ran lightly up the staircase, avoiding the
stately "convenience" of the elevator, and hurried
down the hall to her room. She closed the door behind her and locked it carefully.

At first she couldn't quite make out what was
wrong about the room. Then it came to her.
Everything was slightly dislocated, as if the room
had been taken apart and put together again. Only
the putting together hadn't been very careful.
Drawers were half-opened and cushions over-
turned. The pictures were slightly askew.

Someone had ransacked her room.

Chapter 3

It had to have been Tony's dirty work, Eleanor fumed. He had searched high and low, leaving nothing unturned, and then carelessly, contemptuously shoved everything back together again.

There was no doubt about it, no possible case of mistaken identity this time, because Tony had left a calling card: a nasty little note, reminiscent to Eleanor of those he'd sent her in the old days.

Except that this note was much more chilling than those whining messages had ever been. Eleanor read it, her eyes widening with shock and disbelief:

Sorry to leave things so untidy...just so you know, you and Derek, that you can't get away with a *thing* . Tell him when you see him that I'm very angry with him. Tell him I

want what's mine. And tell him I want it badly, Eleanor.

    Maybe he'll listen to you. If he doesn't, I'm
very worried about what might happen to
him—or to you. . . . Tell him that.

Yours affectionately, Tony

Eleanor shuddered. There was a crazy vicious-
ness about the note that was new, even for Tony.
What on earth could Derek have done to him?
And what could Derek have that Tony wanted so
badly?

Numbly Eleanor moved about the room, checking details. Tony had apparently taken nothing.
Everything that should have been there was there—
at least all of Eleanor's personal belongings—and
she was fairly certain that everything in the room
itself was intact, as well. Her eyes fell on a scrap of
paper—an odd bit of color—at her feet. Stooping
to pick it up, she realized that it was a torn piece of
cardboard from a matchbook cover. On the blank
side, a number was written: seventy-six. there was
no explanation of the number, no other detail.

The scrap didn't seem to mean anything. Eleanor slipped it into her pocket.

She had to think. Tony had gone too far this
time. She should call in the hotel management,
perhaps the police. It was the only way to stop this
harassment.

But she hesitated to do that. She realized that
she was concerned about drawing attention to
Derek.

Derek again! And just where was he?

She had to find him, had to get some answers. If she was going to be the object of Tony's threats, she had a right to know why! Since she'd decided not to call the hotel desk about this break-in, it would be all right to tidy up the room. That would give her a chance to consider what to do next.

Derek had said that he was "between apartments." But her telephone call the week before had reached him, at the number he'd used for much of his stay in Paris. She would try the number now in spite of the fact that Derek had said not to call it when she reached Paris. It might no longer be in service if he had moved, but it was worth trying.

Suddenly, in the middle of putting some clothing in order in one of the dresser drawers, Eleanor stood rigidly still, remembering something.

The letters Derek sent from Paris had very often used only a post office as a return address. He had been deliberately secretive except with the last address, which was an apartment he shared with a girl named...Marie...? *Marisa,* that was it. She danced with the ballet, Derek had said proudly. Only now, according to Eleanor's last conversation with Derek, the relationship with Marisa was over. Perhaps, she hoped, the girl had kept the apartment and the phone. Perhaps she would know something about what Derek was up to!

Eagerly now, Eleanor rummaged about in her traveling bag. The little address book was there, somewhere in the depths.... Out came passport, miniature camera, cosmetic bag, paperback books, notebooks, several pens, brushes, pencils...and then, at last, the morocco-bound address book.

She flipped through it to the D pages and found, among many entries for Derek, crossed out or defunct in years past, one in the rue Jacob.

Eleanor hung impatiently on the line as the hotel switchboard placed the call for her. The phone rang two, three, four times at the other end, and she began to have the sinking feeling that no one would answer. Five...six...seven rings. *There's nobody home*, she told herself. *Just ringing this phone won't make anyone come home.* She was about to hang up when the receiver clicked.

"*Allô?*" The voice was sulky and muffled with sleep. It was decidedly that of a young female.

Eleanor braced herself for another assault on the French language. "Hello," she said carefully. "I am the sister of Derek Darnay...."

Apparently her French was adequate to get across that much information at least, for a sudden torrent of angry-sounding phrases blocked any attempt at further communication. Eleanor waited until the woman had subsided, patiently picking out a phrase here and there that she could understand. The words for "rat" and "criminal" seemed to recur rather frequently.

Eleanor's sympathies were roused, but she must try to get the girl to understand that she needed help. "Please...*s'il vous plaît*...I understand...."

Violently the girl broke into English. "Understand? How can you? How can anyone? Oh, if I get my hands on him, I'll make him so sorry.... Where is he? Do you know where he is?" The last question was suspicious, demanding.

"No! That's why I'm calling *you*. I've arrived in Paris, and he hasn't turned up to meet me as he promised."

"Oh, but I am sorry; it is not your fault. I am just at a loss with him. I am Marisa. Derek and I were together, but not anymore."

"Marisa, I'm Eleanor. Look, I'm sorry you're angry at him. So am I. Do you have any idea at all where he might be?"

"No, I haven't," Marisa said angrily. "I've tried everywhere—his last job, his favorite bar...his friends...I've found nothing! He is nowhere. And he took with him *my* money! Oh, I thought we were happy together...I thought I *knew* him! About one month ago he started to change. He would stay out nights, wouldn't explain where he'd been, and he called me ugly things if I complained. We fought so much! He threatened to leave, and then a couple of days ago he *did* leave. He was gone with *my* cash. I couldn't believe it!"

Eleanor broke in as the girl paused for breath. "Did he ever mention a man named Tony...Tony Belmont?"

"Tony? No, I don't remember that name. Why?"

"Well, Tony is a friend from Derek's past. I suspect that he suddenly turned up in Paris, probably recently, and...influenced Derek."

Eleanor felt the bitterness rise inside. Here was the old pattern once again: Derek making out all right, getting along, even working—and then along came Tony to ruin it all. And a new low had surely been reached if Derek had stolen money from Marisa!

Tony must have finished his prison sentence, then immediately tracked Derek to France. And now, heaven knew what they were up to!

Marisa had apparently begun to weep. Eleanor could hear muffled sniffling over the telephone, and she felt very sorry indeed for the girl Derek had treated so cavalierly. He really was hopeless!

"Listen Marisa—try not to cry. I'll do something—I'll find him somehow. I'm angry with him, too. I wanted to see him very much. . . ."

"Yes, he said that your mama has died, has she not?" Marisa's voice was thick now.

"Yes, she has. Derek is not really related to her, of course, nor to me, but we were very close when we were growing up. . . ."

"Oh, yes, he said so," Marisa said, choking back her tears. "He was truly very sad about his stepmother. I can tell you that. He could be so good. . .I just don't understand!" And she began to sob again.

Eleanor was not about to allow herself to do the same. "Marisa, Marisa. . .please. Don't cry anymore. Have you any idea at all where I might call? Marisa?"

The girl controlled herself. "I am sorry," she mumbled. "Let's see. Here's the number at his job.

He quit a couple of weeks ago, but there are a few guys there he knew. Your French—it is not that good?"

Eleanor was forced to agree. She knew the words, but they didn't sound right. Derek, whose background was French-Canadian, had always had a better grasp of it than she. "No. I have to admit I'm pretty shaky."

"Look. Let me call. I'll be calmer than last time. They are sometimes reluctant to give information to the 'jilted lady.' You know, men. But I'll be more clever and pretend I'm from a new employer or something. I'll let you know if there's anything in it. Give me your number."

Eleanor did and the two hung up. At least now she had an ally. But if anything, she was further from finding Derek than before.

With weary anger she wondered why she was bothering at all. Probably it was that connection to Tony—the idea that Derek had been all right until Tony got to him—and it really was unlike Derek to steal money outright from someone who trusted him. What had they been up to?

Tony held the key to that right now. He was the one who knew what was going on, even if he had himself lost track of Derek for the moment.

I'll confront him, Eleanor thought. It was the obvious thing to do.

But where was he? Lurking across the street from the hotel, perhaps...watching, as he'd threatened to do. Or in the lounge somewhere, behind a newspaper, *watching*....

But there was really only one way he could roam freely about the hotel corridors day and night. He had to be staying at the Hotel Ariana. He had to be registered in a room.

Eleanor called the desk. "Do you have a room registered to a Monsieur Tony Belmont, please?"

"No, *mademoiselle*...sorry," said the desk-man.

"*Merci.*" Hanging up, Eleanor realized that Tony would obviously not use his own name. Then how could she find out what room he was in? The hotel was not large; surely there were only a hundred or so rooms. The clerk would know many of the guests by sight or by description. She picked up the phone again.

The desk clerk was reserved, if polite. "But *mademoiselle*...a tall gentleman with dark hair—that describes a lot of gentlemen, surely?"

Eleanor was glad that this was the day clerk and not the same solemn, spectacled young man who had signed her in the night before. She was distinctly embarrassed, but plunged on. "Oh, please!" she gushed. "You really must help me. I—I find him *so* attractive. I met him on the elevator...I know he's staying here—probably on his own. I just want to phone his room, nothing disreputable, I assure you!" She could feel herself blushing very deeply. The clerk must think her an idiot!

"Ah, romance," he said slyly. "Well, we have dark-haired men, all right. There's one in 104, but I know that lady with him is his wife. Anyway, he is not very attractive.... There's thirty-two, seventy-six, twelve. And oh, yes, a single gentleman in fifty-seven, I'm sure of that...."

Something had rung a small, clear bell. Seventy-six. That was the number on the scrap of matchbook she had found on the floor of her room!

The desk clerk was warming to his task. "There's a forty-three, who is not very tall, but dark, and sixteen...."

"Oh, thank you, thank you so much!" Eleanor hurriedly hung up. She didn't want to be rude to the clerk, but she was filled with real excitement. She fished the bit of cardboard out of her pocket. Room seventy-six! No doubt Tony had dropped it in his haste... or was it on purpose?

Well, whichever it was, Eleanor knew what she'd do next. A little surprise was in order for him.

She collected herself for the interview, checking her clothes, hair, and makeup in the dresser mirror. Square-shouldered, she gave herself a reassuring little grin. *Ready? Here we go to tackle Mr. Tony Belmont on his own turf.*

She let herself quietly out of the room, locking the door, and walked lightly along the hall to the staircase. It wouldn't do to use the little elevator, creaking and groaning her way to the upper floors. Stealth was more appropriate. Glad of her soft, rubber-soled walking shoes, Eleanor slipped up the marble staircase without a sound.

The room numbers on her floor had ended at

fifty-nine, so she calculated that seventy-six would be on the next floor up.

After a few moments of wandering she saw the numbers. In polished brass, against the grained wood of the door, they glinted like a beacon at the end of the shadowy corridor: seventy-six.

Eleanor's stomach tightened a little as she mentally rehearsed the words she would say to Tony. She would walk right up to the door and knock—loudly and firmly. . . .

But she could not believe her luck! The door to room seventy-six was ever so slightly ajar. She could walk right in—startle Tony, catch him off guard as he had so viciously caught her the previous night!

But that makes you a rotten little sneak, just like him, cried an urgent voice within her as she gently, ever so quietly, pushed the door inward.

I have to turn the tables on him, show him what it's like to be spied on, another voice countered.

Her fingers trembled. She *must* have enough nerve. Ordinary rules of behavior—ethics—did not apply where Tony Belmont was concerned. Tony was not an ordinary person!

The door swung inward, inch by inch, on well-oiled hinges. She could hear no sound from within. Very cautiously she moved her head into the opening.

The room was empty with the curtains flung wide to let in the daylight. A couple of suitcases—very good ones—lay open at the foot of the bed. A pair of brogans was placed neatly under a chair.

On the dresser stood a bottle of cognac with an ice bucket and glasses. A tweed sports jacket was hanging on the back of one chair.

Signs of comfortable masculine habitation.

Eleanor summoned all of her faltering nerve and entered the room. She stood very still once inside, trying to calm the almost dizzying sense of wrongness about her intrusion. . . .

She looked around, taking in more details. Seventy-six was a large room with windows that faced the boulevard. There were three inner doors, all closed. The bath, the closet and a third—did it lead to another room? Perhaps this was a suite after all. Tony must be behind one of those doors.

What was she to do now? She'd expected him to be here, to answer her demands for an explanation of the riddle of Derek's behavior. Her righteous strength was fading. Here she was intruding in a strange hotel room like a thief.

But was this Tony's room after all? That briar pipe, resting comfortably in a cut-class ashtray, was unlike Tony. And somehow the clothes were too tweedy, too well cut and the colors were too tastefully subtle.

A new fear seized her. This might be the wrong room! She found herself staring at the tags on the luggage. Would they tell her whose room this was? Or did they have some alias on them, some name Tony was using?

Shaking a little, Eleanor stepped across the room to the bed and picked up one of the tags. She couldn't make out the handwriting at first. Squinting, she slowly read it: Jason Romanel, c/o Samir Marouk, Damascus, Syria.

Well, that settled *something* once and for all. She'd had very recent experience with Tony's handwriting, and this was in no way similar. She had to be in the wrong room! In which case, Eleanor told herself, she must get out immediately.

Behind her a chilling, metallic sound sent her heart plummeting straight to her feet. Unmistakably a door had opened. She was caught. Eleanor's temples pounded as she turned to face the stranger into whose room she had trespassed.

"Do you know, this is just like the movies, I swear it," came a voice.

Startled, Eleanor realized this wasn't a stranger, but the man from the cul-de-sac—the man she had twice mistaken for Tony.

And this time the blue eyes held a glint of ice in them.

Eleanor was flooded with shame. She felt very small and wished fervently that the floor might open up and swallow her. Frantically she searched for something to say, some explanation that wouldn't sound idiotic, criminal, or just impossibly lame. The truth was too convoluted, too bizarre, to begin to tell this man.

But she must say something! The silence between them was leaden, and she couldn't bear the frosty distance in that look. Her foolish brain refused to focus, to make any sense for her out of the jumble of apologies, excuses and irrelevancies that whirled in it.

Then, appalled, Eleanor felt herself begin to tremble violently. Her hands flew to her lips in a helpless gesture, and her eyes welled with hot uncontrollable tears.

The stranger's dark brows rose. "Oh, come now, please...." He stepped uncertainly across the room toward her. "It's all right. I've had my room broken into before...it doesn't matter...." His arm went around her shoulders with tentative gentleness.

The gesture caused the last floodgates within Eleanor to burst. Like a damp straw house all her carefully built defenses collapsed, and she began to cry.

All the grief, disappointment and fear of the past few days crowded in on her and were expressed in wracking sobs, sobs that she could neither quiet nor stop. She wept helplessly, letting it go, letting the man hand her a few tissues; she heard the confused, soothing noises he made, but could not respond. Finally he just held her in the warm, universal way human beings do to comfort one another.

At last the sobs dwindled, gusting back now and then, the way a child's do. Finally they hiccuped to a halt.

She blew her nose and looked ruefully up at him. The immense kindness in his face was almost enough to make her cry all over again.

"Damn it all anyway," mumbled Eleanor.

"That's better. You could wreck your whole foreign intrigue act if you did *that* very often. Here. Here's another tissue. Blow."

Eleanor blew.

"Now sit down. Here, on this chair. Good."

Eleanor sat. He stood a few feet away, hands on hips, watching her.

"Don't watch me," she said, conscious of her red face, bleary eyes and trembly mouth. She dabbed at her eyes and twisted her hair.

"I'm sorry to stare. But you've got to admit that even in Paris few people have had stranger encounters than we've had. Can you tell me what you're doing here?"

Eleanor sighed and drew herself up. "It's a mistake, I'm afraid. A stupid, horrible mistake I made. I'm looking for someone—a friend. I thought I'd figured out that this was his room. When the door was open, I decided to surprise him."

"I see. A . . . good friend?"

"No, not a good friend. Just somebody I know from Canada and wanted to talk to." She looked at him helplessly. That was it, about as much as she could tell anyone without going into the whole sordid story of Tony's and Derek's illegal doings.

"And why the tears, if that's all there is to it?" asked the man gently.

"I'm upset and tired. I've had a death in my family recently—"

"Oh, I am sorry. Look, I won't intrude anymore. Please, just relax. Would you like a little something? This cognac should get rid of the vapors."

Eleanor was silent, so he poured her a bit, handing her the glass with fine, strong fingers. She noticed again his deep tan.

"I've had a death in my family, too," he said quietly. "In fact, I'm in Paris to look after some details of my father's estate. I know how hard it must be for you. . . ."

The brandy had warmed Eleanor, and she smiled gratefully. "Yes, my mother died just a couple of weeks ago. . .I'm not used to the idea yet."

"I understand. No one else can quite know what each of us goes through in bereavement. But you must have other family members to help you through?"

Eleanor hesitated. "Not really, no. For a long time there was only mother and me. No other real family," she said, deciding not to mention Derek. "I came here to Paris to get away, to think," she added hastily.

"Then we are both orphans! No wonder we've been magically drawn together." The man smiled encouragingly.

"Yes," said Eleanor, a little startled. "I suppose I am an orphan. But that's silly at my age."

"And just how elderly are you?" he asked.

"I'm twenty-two," Eleanor said. "But you're even older. Why are *you* worried about being an orphan?"

"I am old, very old. Thirty-two, in fact. And I

guess I can take care of myself. I can see you're feeling a bit better...." His eyes narrowed speculatively. "But I still can't get over it, that I should run into you twice today on the street and now here in the Hotel Ariana. Are you sure you're not following me?"

"Certainly not," said Eleanor rather primly. "I'm staying here, have been since last night. The street thing was just coincidence."

There was that grin again—white and dazzling against a tan that was rather exotic in the gray Paris of springtime.

Eleanor thought of the luggage tags. Damascus. The ancient crossroads of the Middle East. He had come from there, from the sun.

"I'm still rather dubious about finding you here, you know," he said, interrupting her thoughts. "It's very suspicious under the circumstances. What do you think I ought to do about it?"

"Well," Eleanor said stiffly, "you're perfectly free to call the management. I *am* trespassing, and you have a right to do something about it...."

"I would like to make a deal with you, *mademoiselle*. If you follow my stipulations strictly, I won't prosecute." He began to pace back and forth in a businesslike way.

"I think it depends on what your, er stipulations are," Eleanor said dryly.

"Here are my terms," he announced solemnly and held up his left hand to begin counting. "One: You must tell me your name. Two: you must lunch with me. Three: you must spend the afternoon taking in one or another—the choice is up to you, the defendant—of the grand and ponderous cultural glories of Paris with me. And four: We must then have dinner together, even if you shall have become terminally bored with your companion."

He looked down at her sternly, drawing up to all of his considerable height. "There. Those are my terms. I will permit no negotiation. What do you say?"

Eleanor pretended to consider very carefully. "You *are* being excessively severe, you know. In my country the last condition especially would be considered harsh and unusual—but I suppose I've no choice." She stood up and looked him in the eye. "I accept your terms."

He grinned very broadly. "That was wise of you. And now you must fulfill number one. What *is* your name?"

"Eleanor Hamilton. I'm from British Columbia, Canada, and that's all I have to tell you until I'm serving my sentence at lunch."

"And I am Jason Romanel of Vendôme in the famous Loire Valley of France, lately of Damascus, Syria." He gave a little bow, and the crystal eyes kindled with warmth. "It is nearly time for lunch now."

"I'll just go and tidy up," said Eleanor, consulting her watch. "I can meet you in the lobby in about twenty minutes."

"How can I be sure you won't run away on me all over again?" Jason asked.

"I'm an honorable trespasser. I shall stick faithfully to the terms of my sentence, painful though they may be," said Eleanor, sending him a mischievous little look as she left his room. "I'll be there, you can be sure of that."

And she knew she would.

Chapter 4

They lunched in the sort of Paris bistro that Eleanor had always dreamed about. There were chipped enamel tabletops, marble walls and floors, and mirrors everywhere. Old coat racks made of oak held the hats, unbrellas and all-weather coats of those Parisians who hadn't yet returned to their workaday offices. Wooden fans, presumably of Edwardian vintage, circulated the air, which was dense with the smoke of Gauloises and the aroma of fine cuisine.

She allowed Jason to do the ordering. "You're responsible. You set the terms of this sentence," she laughed. They had wine, a light and fragrant vintage, in big glasses like comfortable, round balloons. Eleanor sipped it happily, thinking that this was the first time she'd really felt good in days. Or was it weeks?

It was relaxing to be with Jason. He liked to talk

and spoke wittily with a quality of boyish self-effacement that was very charming indeed. He could be silent, too, but not uncomfortably so. There was something sure about him, something solid. . . .

The anger and fears of the past half day or so seemed far away. Eleanor could hardly believe that less than twenty-four hours earlier she'd arrived in Paris, full of hope, to meet the "new" Derek—and had run instead into the despicable Tony Belmont. Jason, this civilized person sitting across from her, was such a total contrast to the grasping, scheming Tony. She forced the thought of him from her mind. Today she would enjoy herself in Jason's company.

They discussed Paris and food and some of the current movies. They talked about the Loire Valley, where Jason had just rented out his family's home.

Eleanor was curious about why Jason was based in Damascus. "What kind of glamorous work—or play—takes you there?" she asked him over coffee.

"Oh, it's not so glamorous at all, what I do. I'm a veterinarian," Jason replied.

"A veterinarian?" Eleanor was astonished. He hardly looked like a veterinarian. . . but then, what was a veterinarian supposed to look like, she wondered, chiding herself for indulging in stereotypes. Did she expect, perhaps, a little man with spectacles and a white lab coat?

It was just that Jason was so handsome in a slightly rugged, even dangerous, way.

Jason was laughing at her. "Why are you so surprised? Did you think I was an oil baron, or an importer of exotic, but illegal, goods, or a spy? Not everyone is in the Middle East for the same reasons, you know!"

Eleanor felt slightly foolish. "Tell me about it, then."

"I'm part of a team, recruited by the Syrian government, because I'm a specialist...in diseases of farm animals. We're investigating a new disease that's been killing large numbers of sheep in the Middle East and especially in Syria."

"Have you gotten any definite results?"

"We now think it's a viral disease, but we're not certain. When we learn more about it, we'll try to find a treatment that can control it. So far, unfortunately, we've failed. The sheep, you see, are the main livelihood of Syria's wandering people, the Bedouin. If we can't get a handle on this, it means big trouble for them."

"Yes, I imagine there's a whole way of life at stake—values, family structures, everything," said Eleanor thoughtfully. "I've studied the nomadic peoples of North America as part of my anthropology major at university...."

"And have you finished university yet?" Jason asked.

"Well, I have my degree, yes. I was thinking about a career in museum work, and that may require some postgraduate studies when I get back to Canada."

"When are you going back?"

"I'm not quite sure. It depends...on a couple of things. But I'm certainly not planning to stay in Paris long—a week or so at most."

"Then you must be sure to have a good time," Jason said warmly. "Come on. We'll start with some of the sights. Where would you like to go this afternoon?"

"To the Louvre," Eleanor replied without hesitating. "I've always wanted to go there, all my life...."

"But it's enormous, you know—"

"Yes, I know. I can see some of it today and then go back again during the next few days."

"One could spend a year in the Louvre," Jason sighed. "It's an unmatched storehouse of the history and culture of France—"

"And of things plundered from afar," Eleanor interjected very quietly.

Jason smiled. "I don't want to sound like one of those pompous, chauvinistic Frenchmen who always bore everyone to death. Let me just say that perhaps we should set a few priorities and see only a few of the Louvre's treasures."

"All right. We'll see two things. One for you and one for me. What's your pick?"

Jason shut his eyes and pressed his forehead as if to think better. "There's a bas-relief from ancient Babylon," he said, "that's about four thousand years old and has the code of Hammurabi on it, carved under an image of the king and the sun god. I'd like to spend some time contemplating that."

"And I," said Eleanor, "would like to lay eyes on the *Venus de Milo*."

"Wonderful!" Jason waved the waiter over. "Let's go then. If it's museums you like, you're about to see the greatest in the world!"

ELEANOR WAS AMAZED by the galleries, corridors and salons of the famous old museum. They could not, of course, avoid seeing a good deal of what the Louvre held in addition to their specific goals. The incredible richness kept Eleanor in a state of elation. The works of Europe's old masters crowded the walls. Statues rescued from the ruins of ancient Greece and Rome were everywhere: *Nike, the Winged Victory*, soared over the main staircase; lions, elephants and Roman senators lined the corridors.

But Jason led her steadfastly to the room that held the famous statue of Venus. They found themselves at last in the uncrowded gallery.

The goddess stood alone, tall and magnificent in the natural light. Her marble shoulders, breasts and hips glowed subtly. Her face was serene, contemplating some vanished Aegean shore. Eleanor was spellbound.

"They've displayed her so simply—so beautifully," she whispered.

"Yes," Jason said. "It's just right, isn't it?"

"I've never seen anything so fine!" Eleanor said, turning to look at him, her eyes very wide. She found him watching her, his gaze calm and serious. She ducked her head, a little embarrassed.

"Come on, walk around with me. We have to see her from every angle." She took his hand impulsively.

Together they moved around the room in a slow ritual of changing light and perspective until they had arrived again at their starting point. For many moments they were quiet, the warm joining of their hands a natural event.

Eleanor hugged Jason's arm happily. "All right, I think we've 'done' the *Venus de Milo*. On to the next objective, troops!"

By the time they had located the Babylonian relief, and Jason had explained its significance to Eleanor, long, mellow rays of the weak April sun were slanting very low in the windows of the Louvre.

Jason looked at his watch. "It's nearly closing time. We'd better make a quick exit, or we'll get caught up in an undignified general sweep."

"Well, we are not mere tourists," Eleanor said.

"Of course not—" Jason grinned.

"So we'd better beat it *now!*" And out they hurried with less attention to dignity than to speed. Once out of doors they collapsed, laughing, on a bench in the splendid formal gardens, the Tuileries, which ramble for acres in front of the Louvre.

"Two wonderful sights and I'm exhausted," Eleanor gasped. "How does anyone ever 'see' the Louvre?"

"Few do and many lie about it," laughed Jason. "But you can't be exhausted, you know. You have the rest of your sentence to serve."

"Oh dear! How shall I survive? But it's not time for dinner, surely—"

"No, of course not," Jason agreed.

"Can we admire the gardens for a while?"

"Naturally. And perhaps you'd like to have a look at the Seine? Over there is the Pont royal, and beyond it the Ile de la Cité, with Notre Dame. . . ."

Before he could finish, Eleanor had seized Jason's arm and steered him toward the river with its stone *quais*. The evening air was warm and they walked randomly along, pointing at this sight or that, unabashed by any thought that Parisians might find them provincial. Notre Dame's spires loomed just ahead, and across the river were the famous boulevards of the Left Bank.

In the square in front of the cathedral the whole world seemed to be gathered. French-speaking Africans played wild drum music and danced. Troupes of nuns and clergymen lined up for tours inside the old church. Students were everywhere, arguing politics in little knots, or strumming guitars and singing songs in every language under the sun. Artists sat at their easels. And footsore tourists rested.

"Can't you imagine him—the Hunchback— swinging on his bells up there?" Eleanor mused, staring up at the rose window of the great Gothic facade.

"And swooping down to grab Esmeralda from the mob, yelling 'Sanctuary! Sanctuary!'" Jason added with a quick burlesque of Charles Laughton in his famous role. Eleanor giggled.

"I'm glad I'm seeing it with you," she said.

"Me, too," he smiled. "Hey, do you know what time it's gotten to be? It's seven-thirty already!"

"I'm getting chilly. Can we go have dinner?" asked Eleanor.

"Trying to get your sentence all over with, hmm? Well, I'm going to make you linger a bit, but in answer to your question, yes, we can start now. There's a place in the rue des Bernardins, just over the bridge. Come on."

"Should I be dressed a little more formally?" Eleanor asked shyly.

"Of course not. You look wonderful."

And they found themselves for some hours deeply absorbed in conversation. The lights of the restaurant were warm and not too bright, so one had the feeling of being in an old sepia photograph. Only the things in the photo did not remain still; they moved serenely and without haste: the people, the burnished serving dishes, the wineglasses. Candlelight glinted here and there like the little snatches of laughter and conversation that formed the background of their evening.

It seemed that there were endless things to talk about, to share and exchange. But a time came at last when Eleanor yawned as discreetly as she could manage. Jason offered immediately to take her home, back to the Hotel Ariana. Comfortably weary, with visions of all the day's sights and sounds filling her head, she did not protest very strenuously.

They arrived by taxi at the front steps of the

hotel. Eleanor was puzzling over the etiquette of the situation. Should she say good-night to him in the lobby, or would he think he must escort her safely to her door?

They had not yet begun to climb the steps. This was fortunate because without any warning the door was flung violently open.

Three men came out of the Hotel Ariana, locked in some sort of awkward, formalized grip—as if they were all trying to get out the door at once when there was obviously no room. There was an air of tension and suppressed violence about them.

Jason took Eleanor's arm protectively and drew her closer to him.

The strange group of men struggled down the steps. There were sharp commands, a few curses exchanged. Eleanor could pick a phrase or two out of the torrent of French.

"All right, take it easy. . . . "

"Slow down—you're not getting loose this time!"

"It's the police—a couple of detectives," Jason said quietly. "Looks like they've nabbed somebody or other at the hotel."

"Easy, now, Darnay. . ." one of the men said.

Eleanor felt a cold lurch in the pit of her stomach. Darnay! She tried to see the faces of the men. Was one of them Derek?

They were abreast of Jason and Eleanor now. One of the policemen tipped his hat. "Excuse us," he said in French. "Just routine .."

But Eleanor was staring, frozen faced, at the

man in the middle. It *was* Derek! His eyes, narrow and sullen, suddenly widened as he recognized her. He looked very hard at her, signaling silently but unmistakably: "Don't say anything!"

Eleanor's hand reached out involuntarily. The "no" signal came harder and stronger from Derek's eyes. She shrank back, saying nothing.

He looked at her for a split second longer, then turned away as the police hauled him off. The cruiser was there all right, just at the curb. The men pushed Derek into it, shouting all the while.

"Okay, where's your accomplice?"

"Move, you two-bit little crook. . . ."

The doors of the black car slammed, and it sped off, Klaxon blaring.

Jason spoke. "Nothing discreet about the way the Sûreté handles arrests at smart international hotels, is there? Sorry you had to see that, Eleanor. Hey, are you all right? You're white as a sheet!"

Eleanor stared after the police car in silent shock. Jason held her shoulders and spun her around. "Look, it was nothing," he said gently. "Just some petty criminal. Come on, you're worn out."

He guided her firmly up the steps and into the lobby. Everything seemed calm enough. A group of English tourists were talking sedately among themselves, and the clerk at the desk was bent over his work.

Numbly Eleanor let Jason lead her to the elevator.

"What floor are you on?"

"The third."

As they rode up, he eyed her carefully. "Got your key all right? Okay now, here we are. Room?"

"Forty," she replied.

They walked along the corridor to her door.

Eleanor looked up at him, "Jason, I'm sorry, I'm just very tired. Thank you. Thank you very much. . . ."

"Thank *you*," he said. "Now get some rest. Are you sure you'll be okay?"

"I'm sure." She managed a little smile. "Good night, Jason."

"Good night," he replied, turning to retrace his steps. Eleanor watched for a moment, then shut the door.

The room rocked around her, and she was forced to sit for a while. A voice inside her repeated, "So Derek has been arrested. . . ." It was true then, what the desk clerk had said about the police looking for him. A dull ache began in Eleanor's temples. Why had he pretended not to recognize her? Why had he warned her not to speak to him? It must be terribly serious, whatever he had done!

Eleanor's happiness had vanished. She felt nothing but a dark gloom, a sense of hopelessness.

Now what, she asked herself. There was Marisa, of course. Eleanor thought she should probably call her right away, but it was difficult to summon the energy. She didn't relish being the bearer of bad news. Anger at Derek rose within her. A fine welcome to Paris he'd given her, this scene of his with the police, right on the steps of her hotel!

Eleanor wondered what the laws were like here in France. Would Derek be allowed to call her? Could she call him, perhaps? But where would she call?

I wish I knew what's going on, she thought angrily. Maybe she would call Marisa after all. It was probably best to get it over with. She reached for the telephone.

But something stopped her, something she'd seen out of the corner of her eye. She turned to look more directly at what had caught her attention.

An attaché case lay on the chair across the room. It was a tan leather case with brass closings. She had never seen it before.

Slowly, as if in a dream, Eleanor moved toward the case. She reached out with tentative fingers and touched it.

It was certainly real enough. The grain of the leather felt rough; the metal fittings were cool. It was the sort of anonymous briefcase nearly everybody carried these days. There was nothing very special about it—except for the fact that it was here in her room where it had no business being.

Experimentally Eleanor took the handle and lifted the attaché case. It was heavy—solidly heavy. It had to be packed with somebody's papers, but what was it doing here, she wondered.

Something about the case, its inanimate, neutral presence, seemed to warn her, to tell her to leave it alone.

But curiosity got the better of her, and she pushed at the clasp. It opened with a small, satisfying click. She lifted the lid.

Stepping back sharply, Eleanor stared at the open case. In it were rows and rows of currency.

American twenty-dollar bills. Money!

There must be thousands here, she exclaimed inwardly. Her hands shook. Instinctively she realized three things about all that money. One: It had something to do with Derek. Two: It was probably the mysterious something Tony Belmont was looking for. And three: It didn't belong here in her room...its very presence spelled danger for her.

There was a folded piece of paper stuffed into the top section of the case. Eleanor drew it out. A note!

With shaking fingers she unfolded it. At last there was to be some explanation of all the strange goings-on! The handwriting was unmistakably Derek's:

Ellie, please hang onto this until I get back to you. Will call later in the day. This money is payment for a job I did. We can share it! Only watch out for Tony Belmont. He's around somewhere and thinks he's entitled to some of this.

Derek

Eleanor reread the note twice. "Watch out for Tony," it warned. She smiled grimly to herself. And how did Derek expect her to do that? Obviously he thought she would just wait around, dodging the police, Tony, and whoever else might be involved.

But Derek had been arrested! She doubted strongly that he would be calling "later in the day"—or anytime, for that matter.

She didn't want anything to do with this illegal cache, but it seemed she was stuck with it, at least for the moment.

Eleanor's heart sank. She might have known! She snapped the case shut and looked hastily around the room. Where could she put it?

The closet! She stood on tiptoe and slid the briefcase to the back of the shelf, then shut the door firmly.

She felt surprisingly calm. In fact, she decided, I'll just go to bed now and think about it in the morning. She wasn't even particularly disturbed that Derek had involved her with this dangerous amount of money. She felt only remoteness, a cold detachment.

He had gone too far this time. In the morning she would do something about it. Right now she would think about pleasant things and try to sleep.

She thought about Jason. . . .

AT ABOUT NINE O'CLOCK in the morning the telephone rang. Instantly awake, Eleanor picked up the receiver.

"Good morning. This is Jason," said a pleasant voice.

Eleanor felt her stomach skip at the sound of his voice. "Jason! Listen, I'm sorry about last night—I wasn't very polite when we parted."

"You *were* in a daze. But I understand. Don't worry. I've just thought of a couple of things I'd like to see today at the Louvre. How would you like to come along?"

Eleanor thought about the money in the closet for a moment before replying, "I would, Jason, only there are a few things I have to do first. Perhaps this afternoon we can go."

"Don't forget to decide what you want to see."

"Oh, that'll be easy. Perhaps some paintings this time? Can you call me a little later? I'll know then," Eleanor said slowly.

"Fine. After lunch, then," said Jason. "*Au revoir*."

"By."

Eleanor thoughtfully replaced the receiver. If only she didn't have all this business of Derek's to worry about! Jason was so attractive, so much fun. She could be spending her time enjoying Paris with him. He was so intelligent and easy to be with. She let the memories of the day before warm her for a bit as she lay deep in the pillows. . . .

But this wasn't getting anything accomplished, she chided herself. The thing to do was get rid of the money, to see that it went back to where it belonged.

But it struck her with sudden, thunderous certainty that it would be impossible simply to get the money "back to where it belonged." Where on earth did it belong? Perhaps, she smiled grimly at the thought, it really was Derek's money legally. But no. That kind of money had to be gotten illegally, had to be dirty in some way.

Eleanor was filled with anger and shame. It had turned out exactly as Tony had said it would. She had become Derek's accomplice in one of his schemes!

The telephone rang again, making her jump. Already she was behaving like someone who was guilty, someone who was being hunted! She imagined Tony's snarling voice: "I know you've got it, Eleanor, and I want what's mine. . . ."

The phone rang again insistently.

Eleanor forced her fingers to unclench, to pick up the receiver.

"Hello?" she said hesitantly.

"Have you seen the morning paper?" The highly excited voice was Marisa's. Eleanor let out a small sigh of relief.

"Not yet. . . ."

Marisa tumbled on, scrambling French and English phrases. "Derek. Derek is arrested! Oh, I cannot believe it—they are looking for the other crook, the accomplice . . . oh, poor Derek!"

Poor Derek! Eleanor would like to have wrung his neck! "Marisa, calm down . . . what does the paper say? Receiving stolen goods? Well, I guess he'll go to jail this time."

"I am so ashamed. I can't explain to my family," wailed Marisa.

"I'm ashamed, too. Perhaps you'd better just forget about Derek, Marisa. I think he's a hopeless case."

"But what will *you* do?" asked Marisa.

"Go home, I guess. To Canada. My return flight is booked for early next week."

When Marisa's exclamations finally subsided, and she had hung up, Eleanor paced the room, trying to decide what to do about the money.

It really came down to one course of action. *I've got to turn it over to the police*, she thought.

But that was not so easy as it first appeared. To begin with, there was the problem of the accomplice. Wouldn't the police assume that *she* was Derek's partner in crime if she turned up with the money?

It would have to be done anonymously, Eleanor decided. And that could be tricky, too. How could she transport the case to a police station without being seen by Tony? And how could she give the police the money and get away without being questioned?

Eleanor pondered these problems and at length formed a plan.

She would wait until she was leaving the country to turn the money over. It was only a matter of a few days. She would take the case to the airport with her luggage, put it into a locker there, and mail or send the key to the police by messenger. By the time the money was found, she would be gone. And Derek would be left, for once, to solve his own problems, Eleanor concluded with satisfaction.

Right now the briefcase would be better off in the hotel safe than in her closet. Eleanor dressed, and with her heart immeasurably lightened, walked downstairs to deposit her burden with the desk clerk.

To HER OWN AMAZEMENT, Eleanor had little trouble forgetting Derek and his money cache for the next few days.

Every afternoon she and Jason went to the Louvre, and every evening they lingered over dinner in some new quarter of Paris, laughing and talking irrepressibly.

Jason told her about the austere beauty of Syria—of the desert, the mountains, the oases. Soon he'd be going back. His stop in Paris had been partly to await results of tests and to pick up equipment for the crew.

Eleanor described in turn the rugged splendors of British Columbia—the gigantic trees and the mountains, the long ocean beaches of the Pacific. She, too, would be leaving. The time was very short now.

"But it's been wonderful, Jason, seeing Paris with you." Eleanor had seen no need to mention her troubles with Derek to him, and although she'd found herself peering over her shoulder many times, there had been no sign of Tony.

In fact, as long as she was with Jason, Eleanor

felt protected. She was alive with him—a normal, rational human being—and they lived in a world filled with an excitement they seemed to create themselves. Crooks and bad money had no part in it.

They walked endlessly through the city, watching the river barges, the cars and the people. They explored the flea markets and the bookshops. They sipped aperitifs on the boulevards, and they went to the Eiffel Tower.

"I won't forget this week with you," Jason shouted. They were standing at the iron rail of the tower, looking out over the city. The wind gusted at them, and a light rain had driven everyone else inside. But Eleanor enjoyed the rain on her face. She squinted at the sky and let it fall on her.

"Neither will I," she said against the wind.

"I'm sorry you're going home tomorrow!"

She turned to look at him. His coat collar was up, and his black hair was pasted against his forehead by the rain. The crystal blue eyes were bright, and filled with sadness.

"Oh, Jason, I'm sorry, too!" she cried.

Suddenly she was enfolded, crushed against the damp raincoat by arms that were tender in their strength.

"Don't go, Eleanor," he said hoarsely, oblivious to the wind and the rain, and to the comfortably dry tourists who watched them from behind the glass.

"Jason, I have to—you've got to get back, too. . . ."

"I love you, Eleanor." He held her at arm's length, and a wondering sort of happiness rose in his face. "I love you!"

Eleanor knew that she wanted him with every fiber of her being. "I love you, too..." she said very softly.

And so, with the cool rain spattering around them on the ironwork of the Eiffel Tower, they made their plans.

It wasn't until much later that Eleanor remembered she'd only known him for a few days.

Chapter 5

After a brief stop in Instanbul the plane continued on toward Damascus. Eleanor was looking out the window, fascinated as she always was by the changing landscape below.

Now it was twilight, and they were flying over Turkish towns whose lights glittered now and then like small, brilliant diadems in the vast pools of darkness. A few black clouds, the first they had encountered, towered strangely as the sky dulled.

They flew east as fast as the approaching night itself, and the fiery sun spread across the horizon behind them. The lovely spectacle changed as Eleanor watched, and in spite of herself her eyes dropped shut.

She dozed gently, sweetly relaxed in the cradling airplane seat with Jason reading beside her. . . .

Turbulent air jolted her awake again. Jason was

gone. She had an anxious, disoriented moment until she saw him at the far end of the center aisle. They exchanged a smile as he came toward her.

He settled down beside her again. "I went to buy a carton of cigarettes from the steward as a present for Paul. I wired to tell him when we'd arrive. I'm sure he'll be waiting for us at the airport." He put the cigarettes into his flight bag.

"You'll be glad to see Paul again, won't you?" Eleanor asked.

"You bet I will. Paul's a great guy. We're very good friends, and after all the years we've worked together, I have a lot of respect for him. You'll like him, too, I'm sure of it."

"So am I," she murmured.

He turned to look at her. The crystal blue eyes were tender. "You're not too tired, are you?"

"No." Eleanor stifled a yawn.

"You are," he grinned. "You're sleepy. Don't worry. In a little more than an hour we'll be in Damascus."

Eleanor looked out the window again. Here and there through gaps in the thickening clouds she could see long, winding rows of lights.

"I think we must be flying over the coast," she said.

"Yes, we probably are. It's too bad it's getting dark and the sky is cloudy. Otherwise you'd get a better view of the northeastern tip of Cyprus."

She leaned her head against his shoulder, closed her eyes and imagined the islands below...she had images of the yellowish brown earth and patches of Mediterranean greenery, edged by the deep blue of the sea. By the time daylight came again, she would be in Syria, in the Middle East. It was hard to believe: she had turned over a new page in her life. All the fears and confusion were behind her now, thousands of miles away in Paris. It was a soaring, clean feeling to be here with Jason.

Fondly she remembered their honeymoon. After the quick civil wedding they'd taken a trip by car to Jason's home in the Loire Valley. There had been time because Jason's tenants weren't moving in until May.

"I want you to see it, darling, because some day we'll live here—after my work in Syria is finished," Jason had said.

They drove through the magnificent château country to Vendôme, a hundred miles southwest of Paris. The villa of the Romanels, known as "The Primroses," was ten miles or so farther on.

While Jason parked the rented car, Eleanor looked through the wrought-iron gate at the old white house that stood well back from the road, surrounded by a garden just emerging from its winter torpor.

There were a few smaller houses scattered around nearby, and then came fields, open as far as the eye could see. Jason put his arm around her shoulders and said proudly, "Well, what do you think of our house?"

"It's beautiful!" she answered warmly. "I love it already, even before I've seen what it's like inside.

Maybe it's because I know you spent your child-
hood here."

A shadow passed over his face. "When I closed
up this house two weeks ago, I didn't think I'd
come back to it so soon. Then...."

"Then there was me!" she said, looking into his
eyes.

He smiled at her, took a key from his pocket
and unlocked the gate. The path was flagged
with mossy old stones. Privet bushes had burst
into bright, new green, and birds sang everywhere.

When Jason had closed the door behind them,
she took his hand. She understood his feelings on
returning to this house where he had lived most of
his life before going off to college. His father had
died there shortly after suffering a heart attack.
Jason, hurrying back from the Middle East to be
with him, had arrived too late.

"Once father had died, there was no reason for
me to remain at the villa—until now, of course.
He'd have liked you, Eleanor. And I know he'd
have wanted us to spend our honeymoon here,
where he was so happy himself. It's funny, I half
expect to see him sitting in the library—or walking
in from the garden...."

Eleanor gave his hand a reassuring squeeze.
"Jason, it'll take time for you to accept it...."

"Welcome to your new home, Mrs. Romanel,"
he said quietly.

She realized the effort he was making not to
show the sorrow that still lingered inside him.

With sudden gratitude and affection she stood on tiptoe to kiss him.

Hand in hand they inspected the house from top to bottom. Large and airy, it was furnished in a cheerful, casual style with beautiful antique furniture.

After taking her on a complete tour of the villa, Jason carried their suitcases up to a second-floor bedroom.

"Let's divide up the work," he suggested. "While you're unpacking our things, I can set the table and take out the food we brought. How does that suit you?"

"Good thinking. See you in a few minutes!"

He hurried downstairs, and she began emptying the suitcases. Within a short time she had put all their clothes into the spacious closet.

She liked this bedroom overlooking the orchard. She liked the whole house, in fact.

Her love for Jason had deepened daily during their time at "The Primroses." The house was serene, settled, secure. The objects accumulated by Jason's family were simple, but finely made: old books, vases, curios.

The country air was fresh with spring, without the inevitable pollution of Paris, and they took long walks together, drinking in the garden-sweet afternoons. In the evenings Jason would set a roaring fire in the hearth, and they clung together in the newness of their love.

It seemed that nothing could spoil their little world. But Eleanor often had to shake herself to be rid of the strange sense of foreboding that clung to her, waking her in the middle of a sound sleep, or causing her to look now and then over her shoulder. . . .

There was nothing, she had told herself as she boarded the plane, to worry about. The night visitors, the strange shadowing footsteps—all were behind her now. Yet an uneasy feeling persisted.

She wondered whether she had done the right thing by arranging to turn the money over to the authorities anonymously. By now the courier would have delivered the key to the locker at the airport, where she had deposited the attaché case. Soon it would be in the hands of the police, and no longer her concern.

Eleanor stirred against Jason's shoulder as if to physically remove her fears. The airplane was flying steadily, level and silent, into the night over Damascus. She was still trying to shake off her fear as she had so many times at "The Primroses." On those nights Jason would awaken beside her and hold her comfortingly. He did so now, reaching around her protectively.

"Hey, you're having that dream again," he said gently.

"Have I been asleep?" she asked, rubbing puffy eyes.

"You certainly have, my love. We're over the desert, and we'll soon be circling for Damascus."

Eleanor looked down. In the evening light the land below was shaded from blue to red where the sun caught it, with pockets of black. It looked as though some giant tissue paper had been crinkled and folded and then spread out again. It was barren and somehow immensely cold. In Canada Eleanor had been used to flying over countless square miles of green forest and nameless, myriad lakes. That had been called "wilderness." But it had nothing of the desolation of this alien land—this empty moonscape.

The plane banked, and the lights of Damascus came into view far below.

Hastily Eleanor prepared for the landing, straightening her hair and touching lightly at her makeup. If members of Jason's "crew" were at the airport, she wanted to look as presentable as possible. Her mind ran through their names, the ones Jason had mentioned so often: Paul Dumont, Dr. Samir Marouk, Claude Reyssac, Lorraine Gray.

She had a clear mental image only of Paul, who was Jason's oldest friend and a college classmate. Jason mentioned him more frequently than the others, and Eleanor imagined Paul to be a good-natured, optimistic type, perhaps a little bookish. Jason hadn't spoken very much about the others, and their images were vague to Eleanor. It was important to her to get to know them all as well as possible because Jason worked very closely with the group, either at the laboratories in the city or at rugged desert camps. If she was to share his life, she would—to some extent—share his work, too. Eleanor wanted at least to be able to discuss it in-

telligently with him and with his colleagues. The
mysteries of sheep disease were still beyond her,
but she was determined to watch and listen carefully—to learn all she could.

The plane was descending rapidly now. The
lights changed from a golden shimmering mass to
individual constellations, picking out streets,
highways and large buildings.

"Jason, I'm a little nervous about meeting your
co-workers. . . ."

"Hey! Don't be silly. It'll probably be just old
Paul at the airport anyway. He might tease you,
but he won't bite. He thinks he's a devil with the
ladies, but he's really just an overgrown boy.
Don't you worry. You'll love him!"

When they had retrieved their baggage and
gone through customs, Eleanor and Jason saw a
young man with a likable smile coming toward
them. Tall and slender, he had a rather homely
face that was transformed by his dazzling smile
and a free-and-easy manner. He examined Eleanor
with great attention, grinning broadly. He whistled and said to Jason, "Congratulations! You
worked fast, but you made an amazingly good
choice. I couldn't have done better myself!"

Jason laughed and turned to Eleanor, who was a
little disconcerted by this reception.

"Don't let him upset you, darling. I warned you
that he's impossible and has very bad manners."

"I suppose *you* have good manners, standing
there slandering me instead of introducing me to
your wife!" his friend protested. "I'll introduce

myself to you, Mrs. Romanel. I'm Paul Dumont."

"Call me Eleanor," she said, holding out her hand to him.

"Thank you, Eleanor, and it goes without saying that you'll call me Paul. I'm the wisest, most levelheaded member of the team, the one the others all turn to when they need advice. Has Jason told you that?"

"Not exactly," she replied, amused, "but he's told me other good things about you."

Paul's face became serious for the first time.

"I could tell you plenty of good things about him, too. He's a man you can always count on. You're lucky to have married him."

"I couldn't agree with you more," she said smilingly.

Jason was obviously embarrassed by hearing this praise of himself.

"Let's go," he said briskly.

The three walked toward the exit of the airport building. Eleanor tried not to stare when they passed a group of Syrians wearing traditional Arab headdresses.

Outside the air was cool, the sky was cloudy and a few drops of rain were beginning to fall. Beyond the lights of the airport the night was dark.

Paul led the way to a battered old jeep. When the suitcases had been put in the back, he got behind the wheel. Eleanor and Jason were squeezed in tightly on the seat beside him.

"I know it's not very comfortable," he said as he

started the jeep, "but at least it won't take us long to get to the Semiramis."

The Hotel Semiramis, named for a legendary queen of Assyria, was "home" to the French veterinary team. Jason had explained to Eleanor that the Syrian government had promised to provide the members of the team with individual houses in a new section of Damascus, but that so far nothing had been done about that promise. Meanwhile they had been staying at the Semiramis. None of them had any thought of complaining since it was a luxury hotel, and its dining room served excellent meals.

"Has Samir made arrangements for us at the hotel?" asked Jason.

"Yes," answered Paul. "He told the manager you'd be coming back with your new wife. There are two adjoining rooms, each with its own bathroom, waiting for you and Eleanor on the second floor. It's not as good as having a house or an apartment all to yourselves, of course, but it's not bad, not bad at all."

After leaving the airport, which was built on high ground near Damascus, the jeep moved along a winding road. Paul drove with skill and self-confidence and Eleanor was content to remain silent, listening to the conversation between the two men. She peered into the darkness, regretting that she was unable to make out the landscape through which they were passing.

Jason seemed to sense immediately what she was thinking. "It's too bad we've arrived at night,

Eleanor. The oasis is quite a sight. But we'll get around tomorrow. I want to show you everything, all the marvelous minarets shining against the skyline, the orchards and the olive groves...."

"But they're out there in the dark and will have to wait till tomorrow," laughed Paul.

"I can't wait. I can feel it even now—the city's so old, it seems to give off an aura..." Eleanor said.

"It's the oldest city in the world, they say. Here before Abraham. The Pearl of the East!" announced Paul.

"City of Many Pillars," added Jason.

"Yes," Paul went on, imitating a tour guide, "Darned near everybody has lived here at one time or another. The Assyrians. King David. Alexander the Great. The Persians, Romans, Byzantine Greeks. Arabs. And the French. For a while anyway."

"But Muhammad wouldn't come here," Jason put in. "He said it was too much like paradise, which he didn't want to see before his time."

Paul chuckled. "Paradise to some, maybe. But not when the desert wind blows for a few days."

"I thought Damascus was fairly close to the sea," Eleanor commented.

"Only fifty miles away. But the mountains block off rainfall, so we're still a subdesert zone," said Jason.

"I can't wait for daylight—to *see* everything!" Eleanor said excitedly.

"Don't you worry. You'll be marched about until you're ready to drop!" Paul laughed.

"Anything new at the lab?" asked Jason.

"Nothing sensational," Paul replied. "The truth is that we're still making almost no progress. We haven't yet come up with anything better than preventive vaccination for dealing with the disease. Samir has decided to have a massive vaccination program carried out by a team of young Syrian veterinarians. His plan for a research station in the desert has been approved, and the buildings are nearly finished. We'll go there soon. Besides going on with our research, we'll vaccinate all the sheep owned by bedouins in the region east of Hama."

"East of Hama?" Jason repeated with surprise.

"That's right, and it makes sense. Our camp is being built beside the trail that the nomads use for taking their flocks north or south—depending on the season—because those are the flocks that spread the disease all over the country."

"The best solution would be to have those people and their animals stay in one place till we bring the disease under control—" Jason began.

"The government tried that a few years ago, not because of disease, but simply because they disapproved of the nomadic way of life, or at least that's the only reason I know of."

"And what happened?"

"It didn't work. The nomads refused to settle down because they felt it would mean giving up their freedom. So they're still wandering, and we'll have to go and wait for them to pass by if we want to vaccinate their sheep," Paul concluded.

"When will we leave?" asked Eleanor.

"In a few weeks. All the equipment and supplies for the camp will be taken in by truck. We'll leave as soon as everything is ready."

Eleanor made no comment, but for a moment she was dismayed at the thought of going off into the desert. They were all used to it, probably, but she was a "tenderfoot." Then she smiled to herself; she could be happy anywhere with Jason.

"I wish it weren't almost summer," Jason remarked. "I don't like to think of how hot it will be in that desert."

"The buildings will be air-conditioned," Paul reassured him. "Look, Eleanor, there's Damascus!"

The outskirts of the city had just appeared in the glare of the headlights, visible through the fan-shaped areas cleared by the windshield wipers. She could see the ancient ramparts, built of solid stone, with their equally ancient gate. Then came rows of buildings with narrow, barred windows. The streets were unevenly paved with stone. In the distance the spire of a minaret towered above a white mosque.

At the end of a broad, well-lighted street they stopped the jeep in front of the Hotel Semiramis.

The rain had nearly stopped. A uniformed bell-hop hurried out of the hotel to meet them. Jason told him in Arabic to take the suitcases up to the rooms that he and Eleanor would occupy on the second floor.

"Lorraine and Claude must still be in the dining room," said Paul. "You can go and see them there. I'll join you as soon as I've parked the jeep."

After exchanging a look with Eleanor, Jason rejected the suggestion. "Eleanor is tired. I think we'll go straight up to our rooms."

"Without having dinner?"

"We ate on the plane just before we landed at Istanbul. We'll see you tomorrow morning at breakfast. Please apologize to the others for us."

"I understand," Paul said with mock resentment. "Now that you're in love, you don't care about your friends."

Jason laughed and reached into the flight bag that he was still carrying. "Here, this present will prove you're wrong."

Paul took the carton of cigarettes. "Samir intends to give a little party in your honor tomorrow night. I hope you and Eleanor will accept his invitation."

"We certainly will," said Eleanor. "Tomorrow we'll be feeling much better than we are now."

Paul grinned and said good-night and went off to park the jeep.

"Don't expect the royal suite," Jason warned Eleanor as they were climbing the stairs. "In the Semiramis the lobby and the restaurant are more impressive than the rooms."

When she looked them over, Eleanor saw that the two rooms were large and clean but rather cheerless, and that the furniture was undistinguished. There was one note of elegance, however: the matching bedspreads and curtains were made of silk brocade.

The bellhop was waiting in front of the suitcases he had just put down on the floor. Jason gave him a tip, and he left while Eleanor went on silently examining the impersonal rooms that were going to be their home for the next few weeks.

"It's not what you were hoping for, is it?" Jason asked, gently taking her by the shoulders.

She smiled at him. "I told you: 'Whither thou goest....' Really, though, it'll be no hardship. You'll see. We can make it more intimate by strewing around personal objects. It'll be home in no time. We could make the rooms seem more like an apartment by putting both beds in one of them and using the other as a living room."

"That's an excellent idea," Jason said, looking relieved. Then he added regretfully, "I really do wish we could have something better. .."

"It doesn't matter, darling," she said softly. "To me, nothing matters but being with you and knowing you love me."

Chapter 6

A ray of warm sunlight caressed Eleanor's forehead and shoulders. She opened her eyes, blinked
and saw Jason at the window, opening the shutters. It was broad daylight, and the morning
sounds of the city streamed into the room.

"Good morning, darling," she said in a voice
that was still sleepy. "What time is it?"

"A quarter to eight."

"With all that noise, I don't know how I slept so
long. Damascus sounds like a very lively city."

"It is. Come and take a look at it."

She threw back the covers, got up and stepped
into a pair of bedroom slippers, stifling a yawn.
Jason helped her put on a bathrobe, then they
went out onto the narrow balcony.

Facing the hotel, at the corner of the broad
avenue and a little street with dirty sidewalks
brightly lighted by the sun, the open-air display of

a fruit peddler offered bananas, green plums and oranges to the passersby.

Merchants all along the street were crying the merits of their wares; almonds, cucumbers, walnuts and pomegranates were described in rich and lavish terms by the Arab peddlers.

Jason translated their cries. "He's a water seller—the one with the cymbals. He says, 'If you thirst, come to me.' There's a sherbet man. 'Refresh your heart!' is his refrain."

Eleanor gazed out over the city. A haze seemed to hang like the dust of centuries over the square, modern buildings, the domes of mosques, the minarets and the hills beyond.

"There it is—the Great Mosque of the Umayyad—the fourth holiest of the Islamic world." Jason pointed at the marble towers, spiking the skyline.

Eleanor could feel the heat rising from the street as palpable as the voices of the vendors. She leaned over the railing of the balcony, fascinated by the bustle and clamor below. At a nearby public square buses kept arriving empty, stopping long enough to become tightly packed with passengers, then scattering in all directions.

"Is it like this every day?" she asked.

"Yes, every day except Friday, the Muslim day of rest," he answered.

She went on watching the strange spectacle of that intense morning traffic and the teeming crowd that flowed along the sidewalks: men with their heads wrapped in white flannel or wearing the traditional headdresses known as *keffeyehs*; women dressed in Western style or wearing long robes and heavy veils; a child eating a leaf of romaine lettuce as if it was a delicious fruit; a little donkey trotting along the edge of the street, ridden by a fat man whose bulging paunch jiggled rhythmically.

"How do you like it?" Jason asked.

"It's fantastic! When can we go to the bazaar?" she asked impatiently.

"Today. I'm going to show you around. First, though, we'd better have breakfast with the group. Because tomorrow, in case you've forgotten, I have to go back to work."

Eleanor's heart sank at the prospect. She and Jason had rarely been out of one another's sight for nearly three weeks. And now, all too soon, they would be separated.

He seemed to read her thoughts. "It's not all that bad, love. Come on, let's make the most of it!"

She gave him a resounding kiss, in the middle of which the telephone rang. He disengaged himself reluctantly and went inside to answer it.

Eleanor continued to hang over the balcony, happy as a child, eagerly drinking in the sights of the city below her. She watched bicycles and donkey carts jostle with the buses for navigation room in the narrow street. Everywhere there were strange three-wheeled vehicles, sort of motorized rickshas, put-putting through the masses of pedestrians.

Presently Jason returned. "That was Samir

Marouk, inviting us to the party Paul mentioned last night. I accepted for us, but of course you don't have to go if you don't want to...."

"Of course I want to go. I can't keep you to myself forever, can I?"

"Come on then, lazy, and get dressed. We'll attend the obligatory audience at breakfast, and then we can make our escape." He gave her bottom a little whack to hurry her along.

With lightning agility Eleanor returned the playful slap, then skipped out of his reach before he could react.

A mock chase ended in collapse and peals of laughter on the sofa. Then for a moment even these happy sounds were stilled by a deep and lingering kiss.

Jason came up for air. "I think we'd better go," he said huskily, "or we'll be lost for another day...."

"All right," Eleanor sighed. "Give me a few minutes to sort myself out," she said rising.

"You're beautiful already...."

"Well, I have to get *dressed!*"

"Oh, yes, *that* little detail. I suppose you're worried about what the women will think of what you wear?"

"Well, hardly," said Eleanor, her voice coming from around the bathroom door. "I haven't got the kind of wardrobe that would impress anyone. I might need to get a thing or two. It's much warmer here than I thought...."

"Yes, we have the *khamsin*, the desert wind.

It threatens to be very hot for the next few days."

"I'll go shopping then." Eleanor combed her blond curls and smoothed a green print dress over her hips. It matched her eyes; a cool, simple and rather elegant cotton. She would need more clothes, but for now the outfit was satisfactory.

Jason whistled in a low and predatory way as she came back into the room.

"Stop that!" Eleanor said firmly, but she flushed with pleasure.

"My cohorts will be entirely overwhelmed," he said. "By the way, almost everyone's English is good—except perhaps Lorraine's. You don't have to worry about communicating, although they may talk a bit among themselves in French."

"Jason, I'm practicing my accent as best I can...and I do understand most of it. Arabic's what I'm worried about."

"We'll start you slowly. You'll get the hang of it soon."

They linked arms and set off for the hotel dining room.

The large restaurant of the Hotel Semiramis, where the members of the French research team usually took their meals, was on the second floor. White-jacketed waiters moved briskly among the numerous tables occupied by guests from all over the world.

Paul Dumont was already seated at the table reserved for the team. He stood up to greet the Romanels. "Good morning! Eleanor, sit down here across the table from me so we can get to know each other better. Do you know you're even prettier in daylight than you were last night?"

"I don't think Eleanor realizes what an honor that compliment is," Jason said with affectionate irony. "You're not in the habit of being so gallant."

A shy grin transformed Paul's angular face. "You're right...it's been a long time since a woman impressed me as much as Eleanor has done."

Eleanor was blushing deeply. "Please cut it out, both of you. What can we have for breakfast?"

"Let's see," Paul began. "You can have almost anything you like. Tea, coffee, fruit juices. Cheese, fresh figs, bread and butter. Or do you want an 'English breakfast,' with eggs?"

Jason stood up just then, looking toward the dining-room entrance. "Here are Claude and Lorraine."

"Ah," said Paul, rising as well.

The two came to the table. Claude Reyssac, smiling warmly, had been described to Eleanor by Jason as a capable, hardworking scientist. He was solidly built and appeared to be in his early forties. Lorraine Gray was a young widow whose husband had been killed in a laboratory explosion two years ago. Jason regarded her as a skilled, intelligent worker.

"Lorraine...Claude...this is my wife, Eleanor." Jason seemed a little embarrassed by the formalities.

Eleanor smiled shyly and shook hands with them both.

"Well, well! How'd you ever talk her into it, Jason?" Claude's voice was booming and jocular.

Eleanor blushed at all the attention. She hoped they'd soon forget about her and get back to their everyday relationships.

Claude had an affable manner, but it quickly became apparent that he ordinarily kept his deeper thoughts and feelings to himself.

Lorraine was tall and slender, with a delicate profile and a fringe of dark hair over her forehead. It was mainly her eyes that caught Eleanor's attention. They were light gray and seemed to scan the world without finding anything really interesting in it, as if she had never recovered from the tragedy of her husband's death two years earlier. Her handshake had been cordial, but it seemed to Eleanor that her melancholy smile was forced.

They carried on a friendly, general conversation during breakfast. Eleanor was relieved that the "bride-and-groom" bantering was kept to a minimum.

This, then, was "the team," Eleanor thought to herself. Two more members were missing, she knew, but she'd probably meet them that night: Dr. Samir Marouk and his daughter Myriam.

Dr. Marouk, who had been appointed head of the Syrian veterinary research program, worked in close cooperation with the French members of the team. Myriam Marouk had been trained as a laboratory assistant by her father. At eighteen, she was the youngest member of the group. She was enthusiastic about new social ideas, especially with regard to the emancipation of Syrian women.

Eleanor remembered what Jason had said about Myriam: "Physically, she's quite mature, but her maturity in other ways is debatable. She has a complex character—sometimes she's warm and spontaneous, sometimes withdrawn and secretive."

"What does she look like?" Eleanor had asked.

"Dark hair, dark complexion and jet black eyes that make her face intensely alive. Like most Syrian women of her generation, she doesn't wear a veil."

"Do the older women still wear veils?"

"Many of them do, but it's becoming rare among the young ones."

No doubt, Eleanor thought, sipping her coffee, those two would be the most interesting of the entire group.

Jason looked across at her several times during breakfast, telegraphing support and reassurance. But Eleanor felt surprisingly secure. She'd gotten along reasonably well for a first encounter with a new group, especially a group like this one, so tightly knit and unused to outsiders. They were scientists and couldn't stay away from their jargon for very long, but Eleanor survived unscathed.

At length everyone was finished eating and impatient to start the day.

Lorraine left and a few minutes later Paul and Claude decided to go to the laboratory together.

"Why don't you take the jeep?" Paul suggested

to Jason. "You can drive Eleanor around the city and give her a general idea of both the old and the new quarters."

"Sure you won't be needing it today?"

"I'm sure. I'll be at the lab all day, and Claude can drive me there," Paul replied.

"Then I'll take you up on your offer; Eleanor and I will use the marvelous luxury jeep for a tour of the city."

When they were alone, Jason asked Eleanor for her impressions.

"Paul is a very decent and likable man, and so is Claude," she said thoughtfully. "But you didn't tell me Lorraine was so pretty! She seems detached from everything around her. I'm sure she still lives with the memory of her husband."

Jason made no comment, and Eleanor was just a bit surprised by his silence.

"What are you thinking about?" she asked.

He reached across the table and put his hand on hers.

"I'm thinking that I have no right to impose the team on you, and that beginning tomorrow we'll have breakfast and at least one other meal brought to us in our suite every day so we can have more privacy. Don't you think that's a good idea?"

"No, and I won't do it. I don't want to monopolize you. Your friends, especially Paul, would resent it, and they'd be right."

"Paul and the others have to realize that I'm not a bachelor anymore," he protested.

"You've been a member of their group for a long

time. If I made you begin living apart from them, I don't think you could be on the same friendly terms with them as before. As far as they're concerned, I want you to act as if nothing has changed in your life. When I came here, I knew we'd all live together as a group in some ways. And it doesn't really matter since you and I will be alone with each other every night.

"Besides, we'll soon be going into the desert, and I'm sure it won't be possible for us to have our meals served separately there so it would be ridiculous to start now."

"I suppose you're right," Jason admitted. "Even so, I'd like us to begin having at least breakfast in our suite. No one can hold that against us."

"All right, we'll try it and see what happens," she said, smiling. But she was troubled. Jason's reaction seemed to suggest that her first meeting with the team hadn't gone as well as she'd thought, after all.

THEIR FIRST STOP was the bazaar, the Suq-al-Hamidiya, in the old city. They had parked the jeep outside this area of narrow, winding streets and venerable architecture, threading their way on foot through the crowds of deeply tanned bedouin village girls in print dresses and bearded Druze sheikhs.

The market streets were covered by tin roofs or long awnings to protect them from the heat of the sun. Countless merchants displayed their wares in narrow stalls crowded like the caves of Aladdin.

Everywhere Eleanor saw inlaid wooden objects, clusters of painted leather slippers, finely engraved copper articles.

And everywhere there were the heady aromas of exotic spices, of oriental perfumes...the shimmer of brocades, the sinuous gleam of metal and mother-of-pearl. Sounds of happy bargining filled the air.

Eleanor lingered in front of each display, fascinated by the goods and by the people around her. The clothes were strange to her: men wore long hooded robes that hung down to their feet, while many women were shrouded in black or white veils.

Jason helped her choose a low table, inlaid with mother-of-pearl, a chased copper tray and an antique lamp. He haggled over the prices according to custom and arranged for their purchases to be sent to the Hotel Semiramis.

They walked on through the spice market where the pungent smells were mingled with the sweet fragrance of dwarf damask roses, spilling out of fat burlap bags. They were sold for use in making various kinds of drinks and confections, Jason explained.

The couple left the bazaar and came back into the warm sunlight. Overhead they could see the clear blue of the sky once again, and from a nearby minaret the recorded voice of a muezzin called the faithful to prayer.

Eleanor slipped her hand into Jason's.

"Thank you for bringing me here, darling. It's a

whole new world! I almost feel that before I met you, I didn't really exist."

He squeezed her fingers. "I have the same feeling."

They drove to the new section of the city. The broad avenues lined with modern high-rise buildings contrasted sharply with the narrow streets and dilapidated houses of the old city.

"That's where Samir Marouk lives," Jason said, pointing to a hillside on which rose several beautiful white villas with wrought-iron balconies.

He stopped the jeep in front of a large estate, shaded by palm and sycamore trees and enclosed by an iron fence. Beyond the trees was a long, four-story building with barred windows.

"And there are the laboratories," he announced.

"So that's where you spend most of your days, buried in the name of science!" Eleanor noticed a policeman pacing back and forth in front of the gate. "Why is the entrance guarded?"

"Because the building isn't used entirely for veterinary research. Samir's facilities take up only the first floor, and we're not allowed to go to the upper floors.

"It seems that Syrian scientists, and also foreign workers whose governments helped finance construction of the installation, are doing secret research... on a new kind of fuel that will be much more efficient than anything developed so far."

She looked sharply at him. "A new kind of fuel? That means there might be a danger of explosion in the lab!"

"Don't worry," he laughed. "There are all sorts of safety precautions. And there's no testing here. It's done far out in the desert."

"But why hasn't Dr. Marouk been given a building of his own?"

"Probably because the Syrian government can't afford it. But we have all the equipment we need, and we're not bothered by the fuel research. But that's enough about work. Come on."

He started the engine of the jeep. "I'm taking you to the Omar Khayyám for lunch. It's a really famous restaurant, and I don't want to miss this chance to have lunch alone with you. There may not be another one for a long time!"

As they drove through the white city to Marjeh, the martyr's square, Jason explained that Damascus lies in Al-Ghuta, the oasis. The fertile plain, watered by the Barada River, flowing through the city, is sheltered by yellow, arid hills. Grain fields, fruit trees and olive groves thrive there. Grapes, jacarandas and rosebushes crowd the walls of the villas that dot the oasis. And the apricot orchards are famous.

Eleanor could see thick groves of aspens and poplars, as well as mulberry trees here and there. It was truly a garden, a paradise in the desert, she exclaimed.

Eleanor's senses were whirling with all the new sights, sounds and smells of Damascus. At Omar Khayyám they lunched on *fattet makhodons*, the famous Damascene dish that combines yogurt and eggplant.

"Oh, Jason, it's been a fantastic day...I can hardly take it all in!" Eleanor said as they sipped strong Arab coffee.

"I wanted you to experience a little of the city with me before I have to go back to work. You'll probably want to do some things on your own later."

"Do you suppose it'll be all right for me to go about on my own? Aren't Moslem women rather restricted?"

"Some of them still are," Jason agreed. "Many Muslim men do the marketing for their families, and the women pray at home instead of at the mosque—that sort of thing. But the older women are often very powerful in the home. I hear that's true of Samir's wife, though we don't see much of her. She won't be at the party tonight, for example, although her daughter will. Myriam's of a completely different generation. . . .

"Of course," Jason went on, "not all the people in Damascus are Islamic. There are many Christians and Jews, as well. The attitudes toward women vary. I'm sure you'll be okay."

"Well," said Eleanor, "I can't imagine any of them having the freedom I was used to in Canada."

Jason smiled. "Some do. Look at those girls from the high schools in their military fatigues. They're no blushing violets.... You'll be all right—just do whatever you like. This is a cosmopolitan town after all. Don't worry. In fact, I hope you do get out a lot. I don't want you to get bored,

Eleanor. Your happiness is too important to me."
He looked so earnest and so appealing just then
that Eleanor wanted to hug him.

"Jason, I *am* happy. And I'll be *very* busy,
you'll see!"

They drove around in the jeep for the rest of the
afternoon as the exotic new world of the desert
city revealed more and more of its magic to Eleanor. It was just the beginning of her new life, and
it was all an exciting adventure, she told herself
happily.

Eleanor even forgot to worry. The sense of foreboding that had stayed with her since Paris
seemed to have been melted away by the bright
sun that drenched the streets of Damascus.

Chapter 7

Samir's villa was brightly lighted for the party. Nestled in a fragrant garden, it was built with a flat roof and arched windows that showed a certain Mediterranean influence, reminiscent of homes in Italy or the south of France.

The two-story structure surrounded an inner court in the time-honored Syrian way. There lay the cool, serene expanse of a reflecting pool whose basin was shaped in exquisite blue tile. Ground-floor windows and a series of French doors opened onto the court, giving a view from almost every room of the dancing fountain.

Bougainvillea clambered up the walls in astonishing profusion, their pink flowers vivid against the white villa walls. Lanterns lighted the court-yard, and the party guests were surrounded by the rich perfumes of the Syrian night.

Samir Marouk greeted Eleanor with a formal little bow. Slender and olive skinned, he appeared very sleek in an impeccable light suit with a perfectly matched silk shirt and tie. His black hair was streaked with silver.

He announced that his wife was unwell and wouldn't be able to join them. His gaze was very direct—so much so that it made Eleanor just the slightest bit uncomfortable.

"That's a standard excuse," Paul said to Eleanor while Samir and Jason were exchanging a few words. "Leila—that's Samir's wife—almost never comes out when he has guests. She leads a very withdrawn life in the old-fashioned way."

With courteous hospitality Samir took Eleanor on a tour of his house. She admired the richly decorated rooms, the Persian rugs, the brightly colored hangings and the beautiful furniture.

When she and Samir appeared in the doorway of the room, opening onto the terrace, silence fell over the people gathered there. Except for two women in Western clothes, the guests were all dark-eyed young men who worked with Samir. Remembering the description Jason had given her, Eleanor decided that neither of the women was Myriam, Samir's daughter.

Samir introduced Eleanor to the people in the room, then apologized because his daughter wasn't there yet.

"I'm embarrassed and a little puzzled. Myriam is usually very punctual."

He suddenly seemed nervous and irritated. He clapped his hands, and two servants appeared with trays of drinks and food. He motioned to one man and said a few words to him in Arabic. The servant put down his tray on a low table and immediately withdrew. Samir bowed politely and strode after him.

Eleanor looked around for Jason and saw him talking with some of Samir's assistants.

Paul materialized beside her. "You've made a deep impression on these gentlemen!" he whispered.

She realized that nearly all the men were looking at her and felt immediately embarrassed. "Please stay with me," she said. "I feel a little lost in the middle of all these strangers."

"Certainly, *madame*," he said gallantly. "Here, have a drink," he advised, handing her a glass. "It'll help you relax. Don't be afraid; it's made with fresh fruit juice and just a little gin. You'll like it."

Obediently Eleanor sipped. The drink was fruity and slightly tart, leaving a delicious aftertaste. "It's lovely," she said, relaxing a little.

"And try a bit of this Arab nibble. It's made of almonds—with honey and roses."

Eleanor laughed. "If I taste any more Middle Eastern exotica today, I think I'm going to burst!"

"I know. It can be rough going at first," grinned Paul. "Well, what do you think of this house?"

"It's magnificent!"

"Samir is from a rich and noble family," Paul explained. "He certainly couldn't keep up a house like this on what he's paid by the government."

Eleanor surveyed her surroundings appreciatively. Everything was discreetly expensive: the white, leather-covered chairs on the black marble floor, the low tables, the indirect lighting, the oriental hangings that hid the doors. In one corner stood a large vase bursting with fragrant yellow, crimson and blue flowers.

Suddenly one of the hangings was pushed aside, and a young woman in a white dress stepped into the room. Her warm, bronze-colored complexion set off dark, strangely luminous eyes. Eleanor decided she must be Myriam Marouk.

As the young woman's head turned her way, Eleanor smiled. The girl slowly walked toward her a little tensely, but her face remined impassive.

Samir instantly appeared at Eleanor's elbow. "Eleanor Romanel, this is my daughter Myriam. I hope you'll soon be friends."

Myriam bowed stiffly.

"I'm very glad to know you," said Eleanor. "Jason's told me a lot about you."

Myriam seemed unable to answer. Jason had come over to join the group, and he gave her an encouraging smile. Myriam returned a look in which Eleanor thought she saw a glimmer of despair.

"Please excuse me," Myriam murmured. She abruptly turned away and hurried out of the room.

Bewildered, Eleanor looked at Samir.

"Myriam is rather shy," he said with embarrassment. "It always takes her a certain amount of time to get used to strangers. At first she was brought up almost entirely by her mother with hardly any social contacts outside her family. Then I took her in hand and began giving her more experience in meeting and getting along with different kinds of people. Unfortunately she was already twelve years old at that time."

"I understand," replied Eleanor, noticing Paul's detached expression as he stood beside her.

Eleanor thought she understood very well. She understood that Samir's excuse was something he had invented on the spur of the moment. She had just guessed what everyone had been trying to conceal from her: that Myriam was in love with Jason. His marriage must have been a cruel blow to her.

Jason seemed to be absorbed in conversation, as if he hadn't noticed Myriam's hasty departure. *Why didn't he tell me beforehand, instead of letting me find out like this*, Eleanor wondered.

There was an uncomfortable silence between her and Samir, then Paul came to the rescue, saying in a jovial manner, "Eleanor, Samir has a secret recipe for a delicious cocktail. You ought to try one."

Samir quickly seized the chance for a diversion. "There's no secret about my cocktails. They're made with gin and three kinds of fruit juice: lemon, lime and orange. Would you like me to make you one, Mrs. Romanel?"

Eleanor pointed to her glass, which was still

half-full. "Thank you, but I'd rather wait till later if you don't mind."

"There's Claude," Samir said abruptly. "Please excuse me. I have something to tell him."

Eleanor watched him walk away. She turned to speak to Paul, who was fiddling distractedly with his drink. "He knows how his daughter feels about Jason, doesn't he?" she asked, studiously casual.

Paul's mouth fell open. He stared at her, looking uncomfortable and a trifle comical.

"Don't tell me you don't understand what I mean," she went on. "I wouldn't believe you."

"Well, I . . ." he began. The distress on his homely, gentle face was acute. He sighed. "You'd better talk it over with Jason. He can explain it better than I could. Here he comes now."

As Jason strode across to them, Paul discreetly slipped away.

"Hi, sweetheart! Sorry to abandon you, but I needed to talk with the Syrian members of our group to find out how their work has been going while I've been away."

"Of course." Eleanor smiled sweetly.

"You weren't bored, were you?"

"No, not at all. Jason, why didn't you tell me about Myriam?"

He scrutinized her face. A frown knitted his brow, and he looked away for a moment. "About Myriam?"

"That's right. It wasn't hard to guess, Jason. The poor girl looked as if she would have liked to kill me."

"I didn't say anything about it in Paris because I thought our marriage would put an end to Myriam's childish infatuation." Jason glowered into his drink.

"Maybe it's more than a childish infatuation," she gently persisted.

"It's not. Myriam began getting foolish ideas about me even though I did everything I could to discourage her. She's just a little immature, that's all. . . ."

"In Paris you told me she seemed mature." Eleanor, feeling reassured, was teasing him a little now.

"I said she was physically mature. You've seen that for yourself. But emotionally she's still a child. She's spoiled and capricious, and she can't stand having anyone resist her. I'm sure her 'great passion' for me will soon vanish without a trace. I just wish she'd keep it to herself."

"Don't you think Samir might resent you for spurning his daughter?"

"Of course not. He would never let Myriam marry a foreigner, much less a Westerner. I'm sure he's glad I spared him the need for a stormy confrontation with her."

Eleanor eyed Jason speculatively. "Are you sure there wasn't ever anything between you and Myriam, not even an innocent flirtation?"

He laughed. "I give you my word that I never made advances to Myriam in any way, or gave her the slightest encouragement. So don't attach any importance to our relationship—whatever you may hear to the contrary, woman."

He gave her a look that sent little tingles to the tips of her fingers, and for a moment she felt distinctly uncomfortable.

Samir's voice broke the spell. "Mrs. Romanel, may I take your husband away from you for a few minutes?" Once more he had appeared at her side, all politeness.

Eleanor managed a smile. "Yes, of course you may."

"I need to discuss certain details of our work because I'll be away for five days, starting tomorrow morning. I'm going to the desert camp to see how things are coming along. Paul might have told you that we're beginning construction of new laboratories."

Samir's words were apologetic, but his tone implied that opposition was not expected. His eyes glittered under their heavy lids as he inclined his head in a little bow. Eleanor masked her wariness behind another smile.

Jason winked at her reassuringly, then went off with Samir. Eleanor strolled out to the terrace. Lorraine was leaning against the railing, her figure dark against the lights of Damascus that glittered below. She started a little as Eleanor approached her.

"Excuse me, I didn't mean to frighten you," said Eleanor.

"You startled me, that's all," replied Lorraine. For a moment her pale eyes lingered on Eleanor, then she slowly turned her head back toward the nocturnal landscape. "It's a beautiful view, isn't it?"

"Yes, very beautiful," Eleanor agreed.

"Unfortunately this mild weather won't last much longer. Soon the heat will be overpowering; the sunlight will be blinding, and the air and the ground will be completely dried out."

"I know. Jason has told me that summer is very hot in Damascus."

"It's unbearable. That's why rich people leave the city and spend the summer in the surrounding hills. Last summer we were able to come here to Samir's house often, but this year we'll have to live in crude buildings in the desert. I envy you for being able to stay in Damascus and come here as much as you please."

"But I don't intend to stay in Damascus," said Eleanor. "I want to go with Jason."

Lorraine looked at her with a strange expression. "You have lots of courage!"

"Why? Because of the heat?"

"Yes, there's that—and the discomfort of primitive desert conditions."

"If you can put up with it, so can I," Eleanor replied confidently.

"The difference is that I have to, and you don't."

"Maybe I don't *have* to go with Jason, but I certainly *want* to. I'd do anything to avoid being separated from him."

"You're right," approved Lorraine with one of her melancholy smiles. "A husband and wife should always be together."

Lorraine and Eleanor stood for a moment, watching the lights in silence. Two servants brought Turkish coffee and candied fruits. Before long Samir and his other guests began to drift out onto the terrace, where conversation was prolonged far into the warm, fragrant night.

As SHE SLOWLY EMERGED from sleep, Eleanor reached out to touch Jason beside her, but her hand encountered only space. She had a moment of sharp anxiety until she heard the sound of water running in the bathroom.

Relieved, she sank back into the pillows. She tried to analyze what she had just felt. She thought she knew the reasons for her anxiety. When the world had collapsed around her, Jason had turned up, and he had become the center of her life. She had clung to him and rejected the past. Or rather, she had tried to reject it, but it kept sneaking up on her, giving her little jolts of fear. She sighed deeply. When would it end?

Suddenly aware that this train of thought would lead her nowhere, she made a physical effort to shake herself free from the memories: her mother's long illness, the funeral, Tony Belmont's threats, Derek being arrested. She got out of bed and groped for her slippers.

It was still early, and the shutters were closed. The shapes of objects were becoming more precise as morning sunlight filtered in. The warm air was fragrant with the scent of Damascus roses.

In the bathroom the shower had been turned off. Jason was whistling softly to himself as he prepared to leave for the laboratory.

Two weeks had gone by since their arrival in

Damascus. He had resumed his work, and she was trying to get used to having him gone all day. Luckily she had plenty of diversions in a city where everything was new to her. She was especially drawn to the old part of Damascus and made daily explorations there.

She was also getting to know Jason's team much better. She was becoming fond of Paul, who was always spontaneous and open. She hadn't seen Myriam again, but Jason, who worked with Myriam every day at the laboratory, had said that after treating him icily at first, she had gradually become more sociable.

Eleanor hoped that Myriam would be more relaxed with her the next time they met. She didn't want to be the cause of any uneasiness in the group when they went to the camp in the desert.

Jason came into the room, wearing tan pants and a fresh blue shirt. "You're up!" he exclaimed, bending to kiss her.

Eleanor put her arms around his neck and pulled him closer. "I don't ever want you to have to eat breakfast alone. . . ."

A discreet knock interrupted them. Jason went to open the door.

"*Sabah el Kheir.*"

Eleanor recognized the morning greeting of the Arab servant who brought their breakfast.

Jason came back into the bedroom, pushing a wheeled table. Eleanor smiled as she poured steaming coffee into two cups and began buttering the toast.

"When will you tell Samir I want to go to the

camp with you?" she asked after they had sat down.

"I'll try to do it today. He's going to spend the morning at the laboratory. I hope he'll give me a chance to bring up the subject."

"Oh, good. I want to be sure it's settled," she said, reaching for a slice of toast.

"Well, I've had misgivings about having you come with me. You know, of course, that the buildings will be only concrete cubes next to a sheep trail, and more than two hours by car from the nearest village. There's nothing but desert all around—stones and sand, with a few tufts of dried grass—and the heat is overpowering. You'll be alone for long hours during the day, and you'll spend your evenings with the team. Still want to come?"

"Just try to stop me!" Eleanor laughed, undaunted by his grim portrayal of life in the desert. "You can make it sound as bleak as you like, but you're stuck with me—'for richer, for poorer, for better, for worse'—remember?"

"You're a brave girl. And I'll tell you a secret." He leaned close and nuzzled lightly at her throat. "If you'd decided to stay in Damascus, I'd have been absolutely miserable!"

ELEANOR'S AFTERNOON FORAY into the old city had a definite purpose. She was determined to find a certain very special robe for Jason to wear in his off-hours. She'd seen several like it, the loose djellabas so many Arab men wore, and she rather liked the idea of Jason wearing one, the fine white linen setting off his dark, chiseled features. But it must not be plain. Embroidered would be better—embroidered in a certain way, with certain colors, she decided.

She set off confidently for the bazaar. As she passed the pair of ancient Corinthian columns that formed the gateway to the market, she thought of all the sandaled feet that had passed here since biblical times and before.

Hawkers clamored for her attention, thrusting fruits, damasks and copper wares at her.

Eleanor smiled and passed on, searching in the shadowy stalls beneath the awnings. Spices filled the air, and throngs of haggling shoppers brushed by.

The whirl of sensual impressions seemed to sweep her along. The colors of the rugs and the brocades glowed in the dim recesses of the old marketplace, beckoning her deeper and deeper into the old quarter.

She became a little disoriented. The buildings closed in tight, even when she wasn't walking under the awnings. She still had to repress a certain nervousness about being here alone. She passed relatively few women in the narrow, twisting streets, and most of them were heavily veiled. Perhaps the Muslims resented her presence here, she thought a little anxiously. With her carefree curls uncovered, and wearing a colorfully printed dress that moved freely with her long, confident steps, she certainly contrasted vividly against the anonymity of the other women.

Eleanor's mind was racing.

Perhaps they thought her "unchaste." Chastity was the word they used to defend their shrouding and imprisoning of women. Or perhaps they thought her husband less than a man for not locking her inside one of those fortresslike houses with windows only on the second story so that their women might be "protected." The old city abounded with these venerable stone prisons, crowded one upon the next, ancient and immovable.

Suddenly Eleanor shuddered, glad of the incredible good fortune that had seen her born in the West and not in a world where she would be treated as if she belonged to some other species. She did not wish deliberately to offend the Muslims, but neither would she compromise her own behavior.

She walked confidently on through the dim, narrow streets. A turn to her right brought her back to the teeming carnival of the *suq*. She stopped, uncertain of which way to turn. Had she been past that row of stalls already? The little tables of satiny inlaid wood looked familiar but that was natural enough. There were many stalls that sold them.

Then a strange feeling came over Eleanor. Someone was watching her. She was certain of it. The feeling was unlike her self-consciousness at the stares of the Arab men; it had nothing to do with her sense of being a stranger in this city.

Her scalp tingled with a sudden animal fear. Cautiously she turned to look behind her.

Then her stomach gave a painful lurch as she encountered the flat, malevolent gaze of Tony Belmont.

She felt the blood drain from her face. It was a hallucination; it wasn't possible—not again!

He grinned; he looked like a snake who'd just spotted a bird. He stood motionless against the rough stone of an old building. Only his eyes moved: up, down, in a mockery of appreciation.

Eleanor could hardly believe it. Her hand flew to her forehead, touching cold sweat. Her nameless fears crystallized, hardened to the tension of brittle glass. Tony Belmont, following her, watching her, threatening her...in Damascus, of all places!

Casually he strolled closer, his hands deep in the pockets of his lightweight suit.

"Small world, no? Gee, it's nice to see you again, Eleanor."

"Tony, I'm warning you...." The busy kaleidoscope of the bazaar spun away, blurred by the anger and fear Eleanor felt.

"I hear you're married now. New name and all that. Nice move, Eleanor. But you weren't hard to trace, not at all."

"Tony, what do you want?" Eleanor's voice was low and tight. It was all she could do not to shout hysterically at him. She knew what he wanted, though. Derek's money...if it could rightfully be called his. The money she no longer had....

"I'm just here to collect what's coming to me. I know you didn't *mean* to forget all about me when you all of a sudden ran off to the Middle East...I know that, Eleanor. So I won't get rough with you."

"My husband might have something to say

about *that*," Eleanor said angrily, secretly wondering whether he would. Certainly she'd have to do a lot of explaining. . . .

"Your *husband*?" Tony gave an ugly laugh. "I just bet he would. He's a pretty cool guy himself. Really neat, the way the two of you worked it all out."

"Jason has nothing to do with this!" Eleanor cried. "He doesn't know anything about you, or— or Derek. . . ." Passersby stared curiously at them.

"And how would you like it if maybe I told him all about it? I'm sure he'd love to know all the details about your jailbird baby brother, and how you got his loot out of the country for him—"

"You can't blackmail me, Tony! That's not true, none of it. And Jason wouldn't fall for it for one minute!" she said between clenched teeth.

"No, I guess he wouldn't after all," said Tony. "No. . .because he knows exactly what's going on, doesn't he? Your precious Jason is big time, Eleanor. Lucky you met him in Paris when you did. Perfect way to run and hide. Only maybe you didn't know, you dumb little bunny—"

"Know *what*?" Eleanor demanded.

Tony looked at her, his eyes glittering with malice. "So you don't know? Well, I'll tell you. Jason Romanel is the connection. The man from Damascus. *He's running the whole show, baby.*"

Chapter 8

Eleanor stared at Tony in stunned silence. The bazaar seemed to close in around her with its whirl of sounds and colors, closing off thought and leaving only a crazy spin of impressions: the merchants' stalls, the crowds of people and the everlasting clamor.

I'm sure I didn't hear him right, she thought. Had Tony said something about Jason? About Jason being the "connection"? But connection to what?

Tony waited for her to respond, then spoke irritably. "I said, your husband is the man—the mastermind. Where do you think Derek got all that money?" Tony was leaning toward her, his face unpleasantly close.

Jason...the mastermind? *No*, an inner voice argued, *that's utterly ridiculous*. Tony was talking nonsense as usual. With an effort she focused her attention on him. "Tony, I don't know what you're talking about. You've got no right to follow me around like this."

"I've got every right. You've got the money and I want my half. I only want what's coming to me. You can keep Derek's half."

A glimmer of understanding crossed Eleanor's mind. The money. Tony thought she still had it, of course. And now the game was blackmail. He was trying to force her to give him some of Derek's cursed money by accusing Jason of somehow being involved with the whole mess! For an instant she panicked as she imagined Jason's reaction if he was to get wind of these underworld dealings, however unsolicited. . . .

"What have you done with the money anyway?" There was a grating edge to Tony's voice. Eleanor drew away from him. He'd be more than angry if he knew she had turned the money over to the police! He had come halfway around the world in pursuit of it. His eyes held a cold passion as he demanded again: "Where is it?"

"It's not—not here," Eleanor said. The thin outline of a plan was taking shape in her mind.

"Where, then?" Tony's eyes held a glint of triumph how. She had admitted knowing about the money. He obviously thought he had her cornered.

But her only wish was to be rid of him as quickly as possible. She was appalled by this new accusation, this attempt to involve Jason. It was a sick ploy, but it must be squelched before he could get to Jason and spread his venom over the happiness of their marriage.

"All right," Eleanor said, stalling desperately. What could she tell him? Anything, obviously, to gain time for a few days. After that she and Jason would be gone with the team to the desert camp near Hama. Tony could not follow them there.

Tony moved impatiently toward her. "Tell me, Eleanor. I haven't come all this way just to be put off. Derek's in jail out of my reach, but you're not. You've got no way out. I could pass on the dope about your husband's activities, you know. I could tell the Syrians what he's up to. They wouldn't like it, Eleanor."

Eleanor was thoroughly repelled. But she needed time. "And just what is he up to, Tony?"

"Smuggling. Big-time smuggling. He brought something into France and passed it on to Derek. Derek and I were supposed to split the money, but he got secretive. Wanted it all to himself. I don't know what the stuff was...drugs, maybe."

In spite of herself Eleanor felt a cold tingle in her spine. Jason couldn't be mixed up in drugs!

Tony went on: "I had to watch closely. It all centered on the Hotel Ariana. The man from Syria was in room seventy-six, and Derek went there for the stuff...."

Room seventy-six...that had been Jason's room! Could there be a connection? It didn't seem possible!

Tony was still talking: "...and Derek tried to cut me out of the deal. I didn't know quite what was going on at first. He lied to me. But I figured it out soon enough. And it was just too damned neat, you marrying the guy. Then I knew I was right. You're all in it together, and you'd better come across, Eleanor, or I'll go to the local authorities. I understand they don't treat drug smuggling lightly in this part of the world. . . ."

Quickly Eleanor lied. "Look, the money's in a safety-deposit box. In a bank."

"Have you exchanged the U.S. currency?"

"No, I—"

"It doesn't matter," he interrupted. "I'll take care of that. Congratulations, Eleanor. I wasn't sure you'd have the nerve to smuggle such a large amount of money into a foreign country. But I suppose it wasn't too hard to slip a little attaché case into a crate full of laboratory equipment. Just the way your husband gets stuff *out* of the country, right?"

"Wrong!" Eleanor said angrily. "I told you—my husband is *not* involved. I did it for Derek—to keep the money safe."

"Like hell," sneered Tony. "Well, it doesn't matter to me one way or the other just as long as I get my cut. I don't know how your husband does it, but my contacts in Paris are sure of one thing: there's something big going on here. Drugs, that's what it had to be. Somebody here, getting the stuff over the border from Afghanistan, then taking it on to Europe. Somebody with a good cover. Somebody like Jason Romanel."

Eleanor's thoughts became icy clear. If Tony believed Jason was some kind of international crook, he would make as much trouble as he could. She would get rid of him though, easily enough. "Just forget about Jason, Tony. Do you want the money, or don't you?"

"Now you're talking sense." His malevolent grin made Eleanor tremble with rage. But she held herself carefully in check. "You've got to wait a couple of days."

"Forget it!"

"You've got no choice, Tony. The banks here are closed because it's a Muslim holy day. Then there's the weekend. We have to wait until Monday."

Tony glared at her. "I don't trust you."

"You'll have to trust me. And you'll have to stay out of sight. I won't cooperate at all if you so much as show your face at the hotel—or anywhere else. Understand?" Inwardly she prayed he wouldn't see through her bluff.

He looked defiant, but said nothing.

"I'm telling you, Tony. I'll give you the money. But I won't have you slinking around, threatening me."

"How do you expect me to last until Monday? I spent all my money getting here and on 'research' into your activities."

Eleanor reached into her purse. "All right. I'll give you a down payment." She thrust a handful of Syrian currency at him. "There. That'll keep you in style, Tony. Now then, I'll meet you on Monday to give you the rest. Ten-thirty in the morning in front of the Great Mosque. Okay?"

Tony hastily folded the money into his pocket and scowled at her. *"Be* there."

"Oh, I'll be there," Eleanor said. She tried to keep her face straight. She would be at the desert camp on Monday—far out of Tony's reach! A sense of relief flooded her. He was falling for it; she would be rid of him, and that was all that mattered! "I'm going now, Tony. And don't bother to follow me."

And she walked confidently away, never looking back.

Threading her way through the marketplace, she came at last to the ancient gates. She joined a crowd of passengers in one of the shared taxicabs of Damascus and headed back to the hotel. All the way back she fought to dismiss Tony from her mind. There was no need to tell Jason about the encounter, nor about the bizarre accusations Tony had made. Tony could wait in front of that mosque on Monday, counting his rotten little chickens that would never hatch. She was free of him, and that was that.

WITH JASON SHE HAPPILY packed for Hama and the camp in the desert.

"How will we get there?" Eleanor asked.

"Our baggage will be sent by truck, and we'll go in cars. It's not a very long trip...about 150 miles."

"Do you know the Hama region?"

"A little. Paul and I drove there in the jeep when we first came to Syria. Part of the Hama plain is

watered by the Orontes River, but unfortunately
the camp is beyond that fertile area. It's right on
the trail used by the bedouin nomands past Sele-
miye. That's where we need to be for our work.
We'll stay there for some weeks—or maybe
months—until we're finished."

"Is the disease still spreading?" she asked in-
terestedly.

"Yes. So far all we've been able to do is slow it
down. Infected sheep are scattered all over the
country. A hundred thousand have already died
in the northwest. The province of Aleppo has had
the greatest losses because it's the center of the
sheep trade."

"Do you think you'll be able to isolate the cause
of the disease?"

"Our progress has been slower than we expected, but we're headed in the right direction. Someday we'll succeed."

"I'm proud to be married to a scientist who's
doing such valuable work," said Eleanor, very
seriously.

Jason laughed. "I think of myself as a practical
veterinarian, not as a scientist. But I'm flattered all
the same."

THE CAMP IN THE DESERT was just as Jason had
described it: three buildings around a small pool
of water where bedouins brought their flocks to
drink. A few stunted trees and thorny bushes completed the landscape. On either side of the trail
that stretched away to the horizon in both di-

rections there was nothing but sand, stones and thin tufts of grass struggling to stay alive in the dry heat. Even the bare hills failed to break the monotony of the sunbaked landscape.

To the east was the yellow vastness of the desert. To the west, an hour or two away by car, was the city of Hama. Now and then a hot wind raised whirls of dust; otherwise, the desert was very still.

"An earthly paradise," remarked Paul as he got out of the car. His face was melancholy as he surveyed the bleak landscape.

"Well, let's go and see if the inside matches the outside," said Eleanor good-naturedly.

The longest of the buildings was divided into three parts. The first part contained the laboratory, whose equipment and construction Samir had personally supervised; the second was a room where sick sheep could be examined; the third part contained the generator, which provided power for light, air-conditioning and refrigeration.

In one of the two other buildings were the kitchen and the large dining room where the team members would take their meals together. The cook, who had been hired in Damascus, was to take over the kitchen that evening.

The remaining building contained only bedrooms and bathrooms, connected by a wide hall. With their new, but scanty, furniture, the rooms were rather Spartan and austere. Mosquito netting was hung in the windows, keeping the rooms in semidarkness.

The Romanels and Paul completed their tour in glum silence, but Paul's basic optimism couldn't be quelled for long. "It's not the Hotel Semiramis, of course, but it has its advantages," he grinned.

"And what might they be?" asked a skeptical Jason.

"For one thing, there won't be any traffic noises to keep us awake at night. Furthermore, we can be sure the view won't be blocked by people putting up new buildings."

"Some view," remarked Eleanor, drawing back the netting at the window. "Oh, look!" In the distance, strung out along the trail, was a flock of sheep. Two overloaded camels ambled along in their strange, stately way, led by nomads wearing *kaffiyehs*. A couple of donkeys followed with the women and children. Behind the procession the wind scattered clouds of dust.

"First customers," announced Paul. "I wonder if they have any sick sheep."

As it turned out, they did. Three sheep had already died, and of the thirty or so remaining, six were seriously ill. The animals moved laboriously, showing symptoms of the disease that would kill them within a few days: red, watering eyes; swollen tongues, lips and legs.

The Bedouins said they were fleeing from the north where the disease was rampant. They didn't seem to realize that things were no better in the south. Using their limited Arabic, Jason and Paul explained why they were there and advised the nomads to set up camp nearby to avoid the risk of spreading the disease. They were told they should not leave without having their sheep examined.

Mistrustful, the nomads hesitated, arguing among themselves. Fortunately Samir and the rest of the team drove up at that point, and Samir was able to convince the bedouins to stay.

Eleanor was too tired to unpack. She watched the bedouins slowly raise their big tent, made of camel hides sewn together. Two families would have shelter inside. Around it the children played in the light of the setting sun while Claude, Paul, and Jason set about examining the sick sheep.

The remainder of the flock gathered for the night, guarded by a vigilant dog whose color blended with the sand. Then the sun disappeared behind the hills, and darkness settled over the camp.

The work at the camp was intense and physically demanding. But it was also more rewarding. Here, laboratory research was augmented by practical experience with the diseased animals. Sheep too sick to be saved were killed and buried deep in the sand. The pool from which the animals drank was sterilized every day. In spite of these efforts progress was very slow. The strain on the team members became quickly apparent. They were racing against time now.

The air-conditioning in the buildings was inadequate, and the workers suffered from the heat, which was especially intense from ten in the morning until five in the afternoon. They often worked late into the evening, after dinner, to take advantage of the cooler hours. The team members seemed to keep a high level of morale in spite of poor conditions. They worked together well. Eleanor, though she wasn't part of the group, contributed whatever she could, often typing Jason's notes for him in the evenings.

Myriam never sought Eleanor's company, but she was at least polite when circumstances brought them together. Life seemed to settle into a fairly normal routine without interruptions, except for the shifting populations of bedouin tribesmen.

Eleanor felt a sort of subdued triumph when she remembered her last encounter with Tony. She could not help cringing a little sometimes when she thought of his anger at discovering her trick— but it was only a fraction of what he deserved, and she commended herself for having handled the situation well...under the circumstances.

In the evenings while the team worked in the lab, Eleanor would occasionally sit outside, watching the pale glow of the lanterns in the bedouin tents and listening to the dogs that barked dismally into the desert silence. Often alone like this, she was free to think.

Now and then, however, during those evenings when the stars seemed to fall down, ready to touch the earth, Tony's words would surface in her memory: "Jason Romanel is the connection, the man from Damascus." The idea was absurd, of course. But there was one small thing that kept nudging at the corner of Eleanor's mind. It was the matchbook, the scrap of paper she had found in her room at the Hotel Ariana. The one with seventy-six written on it. Seventy-six had been Jason's room number...but how could she doubt Jason's honesty? She trusted him completely and implicitly.

And yet he had lied, at least by omission, about Myriam. But that had been such an insignificant matter. Still, her mind went back to the room numbers. A coincidence, just a small coincidence.

The man from Damascus had stayed in room seventy-six at the Hotel Ariana. Jason had stayed in room seventy-six at the Hotel Ariana. Jason had come from Damascus.... Eleanor shook off the thought. Jason was a veterinarian. He was obviously dedicated to his work. He was not an international criminal.

And yet *somebody* from Damascus had been involved in the deal that Derek had made—whatever dirty deal that had been—to get his hands on all that money. But it *was* a coincidence, she reassured herself.

It was not, reflected Eleanor one evening as she watched the starry night, a small coincidence at all. It was a large coincidence. *If* Tony could be believed.

After all, he hadn't been terribly sure of himself. Tony hadn't really known what the deal was about, wasn't sure just what was being smuggled, or how, or by whom.

Was it drugs? An obvious guess. Eleanor considered the matter deeply for a moment. If not drugs, then what could possibly be so valuable, cause so much money to change hands?

Suddenly Eleanor shuddered inwardly. Derek would never forgive her for turning "his" money in. But she had tried not to think of that all along. He should never have saddled her with his loot—and losing it would teach him a permanent lesson—perhaps.

Eleanor was tempted to tell Jason about Derek and the money, about Tony and the rest of it. But she was also reluctant to explain any of it...it was just too sordid. No, she decided, far better to let it pass and simply trust the case was closed.

And, she realized now, there was another reason. She had married Jason so quickly that she herself had suppressed an inkling that the marriage was at least partly an escape for her—an escape from her worries and from the grasping, clinging memories. Might Jason not think the same thing—that she'd married him only to escape? Eleanor knew him well enough by now to realize that he had a certain sensitivity and lack of assurance about her love. It was charming and rather sweet...but it made her very careful about hurting his feelings.

Eleanor sighed. If only Jason were not so busy these days. The team was working frantically on the increasingly serious problem of the sheep virus. Jason came to their quarters late at night, invariably exhausted. There was no time to discuss the knotty problems of the past.

Later on perhaps, when their marriage had settled into some kind of routine...then she would have time to really get to know Jason and to confide in him all her uncertainties and fears. Right now his work was more important.

Eleanor had been trying particularly hard to be useful to the team. She fetched and carried and typed reports, but her university training did not adapt her very well to the work, either with the animals or in the lab. She felt increasingly like an outsider—and an almost useless one at that.

Jason had become withdrawn, steadily less communicative, as the pressure to solve the virus mounted. Eleanor told herself that her chief concern ought to be helping him to relax.

Eleanor watched the last lights go out in the tents of the bedouins. She reflected that their simple lives, though filled with the never ending struggle against the hardships of the cruel desert, had a dignity that anyone might envy. The pressures of city living were held in contempt by the bedouins. They loved their proud wandering life on the desert plateaus and could not imagine why town dwellers would want to toil day after day just to stay in one place!

She had visited the bedouin tents with Jason and had been amazed. They seemed to live contentedly with so few possessions: mats, pillows, a couple of utensils...and the lamps that were dimmed now.

Eleanor knew the laboratory lights would not go out for some hours. She decided to go over and see if there was anything she could do. She didn't want to be in the way, but there must be something useful she could do.

Her thoughts were interrupted by soft footsteps in the darkness behind her.

"Don't jump," said Paul. "It's only me!"

"Paul! You did startle me," Eleanor replied a little shakily. "It's so quiet out here."

"I know...it must be very difficult for you, having to hang around all by yourself while we work half the night...."

"No, really, I don't mind a bit. I only wish there was more I could do, that's all."

"You've done a great deal. And you're very good for Jason, you know."

"I hope so. He's so quiet lately."

"He's just worried. Professional problems. Now tell me, Eleanor, what's on *your* mind? You did jump about a mile when I lumbered up behind you."

"There's nothing on my mind, Paul. I was just sort of thinking, wondering about the country we're in...." Eleanor took a deep breath. "Have you heard of much smuggling going on in and out of Syria?"

Paul looked a little startled. "Smuggling? What kind of smuggling? Persian rugs, arms, white slavery? I mean, I suppose there's plenty of the usual stuff going on...."

"What about drugs?" she asked softly.

Paul grinned. "A little intrigue to ease the boredom, huh? Well, perhaps you'll get a break soon. I understand Jason's going into Damascus in a day or two."

"He hasn't mentioned it," Eleanor replied "Why is he going?"

"Over the past while, Jason seems to have been appointed chief traveler and courier for the team. Whenever we need new equipment, or samples processed, he's the one to go. This time I think he needs to use the big electron microscope back at the lab. He may be onto something with this virus, and he's running special tests, I guess. It might mean a few days at Samir's house for you."

Damascus! That was the last place Eleanor wanted to go. What if Tony was still hanging around? A clammy fear stole over her. She couldn't go to Damascus with Jason. . . .

"You don't seem very pleased," Paul said, watching her closely.

"I'm all right, really. It sounds like a wonderful idea." Eleanor smiled as brightly as she could manage.

"Good. It'll get you away from this grim outpost, and that's what you need. And don't worry about Lorraine. She's feeling better."

"Lorraine?" Eleanor had started to go inside, but now she stopped and turned to look at Paul. "What's wrong with Lorraine?"

Paul looked suddenly very embarrassed. "Oh, Lord, I forgot. You didn't know!"

"What didn't I know?"

"Well," Paul faltered. "Okay. Lorrain's had a time of it over you and Jason. She used to sort of—be with him, you see. There were a couple of scenes in the lab, but she's calmed down now. I feel like a rat, letting you find out. I'm sorry." His expression was one of acute distress.

Eleanor's response was carefully offhand. "Don't be silly. Can my husband help it if his charm is absolutely fatal? I don't blame Lorraine—or Myriam. I married him after one week in Paris, didn't I?"

Paul looked immensely relieved. "Eleanor, you're a sensible girl. I know it means nothing that he didn't tell you. He probably just didn't want to upset you, that's all."

Probably, Eleanor thought. *But that's the second past romance he hasn't told me about.* It would be different if she didn't know the women, if she didn't see them every single day of her life, Eleanor told herself.

"Come on," Paul urged, suddenly cheerful. "Let's head back to the dining room and mix some cocktails for the weary slaves, huh? They'll soon be coming off shift."

"Right!" said Eleanor. She tried to inject enthusiasm into her response, but her mind was careening from image to image: Jason with Lorraine; Jason with Myriam; Jason with her. Was he some sort of Don Juan?

She heard her own ironic words: "I married him after one week in Paris, didn't I?" She had indeed! Was it possible that she'd been a complete fool to marry a stranger against every piece of advice she'd ever received on the subject? It was highly possible! She had only begun to know Jason. Perhaps there were more secrets beneath that handsome facade. . . .

Resentment welled up within Eleanor in spite of her attempts at self-control. Why hadn't he told her about all these women in his past? Obviously she didn't know Jason Romanel nearly as well as she had thought!

But she had little time to absorb the new information. Paul had her by the elbow and was steering her into the dining hall. The team was gathered there, looking frayed after a very long day and an even longer evening.

"That was the worst ever!" moaned Claude to general assent. Eleanor smiled resolutely at all of them, shedding what she hoped was special warmth on Myriam and Lorraine. Samir had not yet arrived.

"I'm taking orders for nightcaps," announced Paul, "so you'll all sleep well."

Everyone groaned, protesting that sleep would be no problem whatsoever. But they accepted the drinks Paul prepared.

Jason quietly slipped an arm around Eleanor's waist. "Hi, stranger," he said with a weary smile. Eleanor gave him a little squeeze. Stranger? Who was the real stranger, she wondered, still feeling piqued by jealousy.

Samir's voice came from the doorway. They all turned toward him. He stood there, impeccable and courtly as usual. "Good. I am glad to see you relaxing at last. I have someone with me—a guest. He is a traveler, lost in the desert, with whom we shall share our refreshments." He turned to the doorway.

"Come, come in, please. You are more than welcome."

The man entered the dining hall, wearing dusty fatigues and smiling apologetically while Samir explained his predicament: a broken-down jeep, disabled less than a mile away; he'd seen their lights and followed the sheep path to the camp on foot. Samir began to introduce him to the circle of team members. "This is Jacques Chessy, a countryman of yours and a journalist." And he began to give the names of the group members in turn.

But Eleanor heard little of what Samir was saying. There was a strange roaring in her ears, and she stood very still, staring fixedly at the man in dusty khaki. She squeezed Jason's arm very tight, seeking some sort of hold on reality—any reality. . . .

Oh, God, not again, a voice inside her whispered.

"Jacques Chessy" was Tony Belmont!

Chapter 9

She cornered Tony the next morning, immediately after the team had gone off to the lab. She had suffered the sardonic stare of those hard eyes for at least an hour the night before and had listened in frozen silence to his preposterous stories about being a newspaperman. She had lain awake most of the night, remembering his threats. And she had heard the smooth litany of lies again this morning over breakfast.

Eleanor had had enough.

She tracked him down as he was strolling confidently through the camp, surveying the installation for all the world as if he was actually interested in writing an article on the team's work. They had believed him, had welcomed the idea, had urged him to stay. Eleanor was determined to have it out with him...to see that he did *not* stay.

She began without preamble. "All right, Tony. I know why you're here."

He turned to look at her, a malicious gleam in his opaque eyes. "Sure you do. I ought to fix you good, Eleanor, for that little trick you played on me in Damascus."

"You won't get that chance," she replied grimly.

"Don't worry. You're too valuable, kid. I wouldn't hurt you, not now."

"You won't hurt anybody, Tony. I've had enough of your games. I should have told you then, but I'm telling you now: I lied to you about the money. I haven't got it. I didn't bring it to Syria. I only had it for a few hours in Paris—because Derek forced it on me. But I didn't keep it. I turned it over to the police." Eleanor's voice rose a little in spite of her steely, clipped speech. "The *police* have it, Tony—in Paris! The money's gone, so you might as well go, too."

Tony's stare was cold, unwavering. "I hope you don't think I'm worried about such trifles any longer," he said. "As far as I'm concerned, you may very well have turned the money over to the Paris police.

"Although I somehow doubt it," he added with a thin, infuriating smile. "But I've raised the ante, I'm afraid. You and your husband are going to have to pay a lot more than a few thousand to keep me quiet."

There it was again: the infuriating, stupid accusation against Jason!

"Tony, I've *told* you: there's nothing to keep you quiet *about. . . .*"

"Oh, but there is, Eleanor, there most certainly *is*. No wonder you dodged out on me in Damascus. You knew I didn't have the *real* story. You thought you were safe, right? But I've got it now, Eleanor, all of it. Your husband stands to make millions out of this deal. Except now, it all depends on me. Because if I blow his cover to these Arabs, that'll be the end of the deal—and the end of him."

Eleanor sighed wearily. "Tony, just what are you talking about?"

"There's nothing you can do, Eleanor, but cooperate. I'm not letting you out of my sight again. You're going to arrange the whole thing, my two hundred thousand—"

In spite of herself, Eleanor gasped. "Two. . . hundred. . . thousand?"

"Sure. What he stole is worth millions. I'm being very reasonable."

"Millions? What could Jason have possibly 'stolen' that could be worth millions?"

"If you're determined to play dumb, Eleanor, go right ahead. But I'll give you a clue, just so you'll know I'm not kidding this time. It had to do with the lab in Damascus. What do you suppose they were making upstairs?"

"Upstairs? Why, that's where the fuel research was being done. . . . You mean that was something there to steal?"

"Exactly, sweetheart. Didn't you ever notice the

guards out front? Well, I checked with some friends in Paris, and they came up with a story going the rounds about a certain formula, developed in Syria...."

Eleanor was bewildered. "A formula?"

"Right. A formula for fuel, Eleanor. A formula to replace fossil fuel—that's *oil* to you. The Arabs were anxious to develop it because one day they'll run out of oil like everybody else. The Arabs kept a cloak on the whole thing—or so they thought. They claimed that 'research' was still in progress. But all the time everybody knew that they'd come up with it. And there were plenty of people in the West who would pay very big money for that formula, Eleanor. Your husband knew that. He used his position at the lab to get hold of it somehow and took it to Paris. Derek got thousands just for being a runner and carrying a piece of paper from seller to buyer. Nobody knows who bought the formula, except that they're very, very rich. The man from Damascus got plenty of money on the deal."

"But Jason hasn't got any money," Eleanor protested.

"Of course not! Why would he flaunt it? He needs to stick to his role of humble biologist, or veterinarian, or whatever he is. He had to keep his cover for a while. Probably the Syrians don't even know yet their formula is gone. He's obviously tucked the money away somewhere safe like Switzerland, which is why I'm here—"

"How do you know all this?" Eleanor demanded. It was all so farfetched, straight out of some cheap adventure story....

"I told you. I have excellent contacts. And I've kept my eyes open during my extended stay in Damascus. It wasn't hard to figure out. The Paris end of it was easy enough to get."

He looked so smug, so pleased with himself. Eleanor was bursting with fury. "I don't believe you! I don't believe my husband would *ever* be involved with such things."

"Well, it would be impossible with anyone else, but I'm beginning to think you really are the dumb little goody-goody you let on you are! Maybe he hasn't told you anything...maybe Derek really didn't tell you anything, either." Tony laughed. It was an ugly sound, dry as the desert air that suffocated Eleanor through her rage and dismay.

"Just how well do you know this guy you married anyway?"

Eleanor stared at Tony defiantly, but no words would come.

He laughed again in his humorless way. "Well, you know about him now, don't you? And you're going to tell him I mean business. I want two hundred thousand dollars. *Then* I'll go away and leave you alone."

Tony's eyes glittered. They seemed to be polished like cold metal. For a moment Eleanor could not tear her gaze from his. It was as if she were some small animal, caught and mesmerized by a beast of prey. Her head was whirling with these new accusations, these demands, the staggering amounts of money...

With a powerful effort of will she at last unlocked her eyes from his stare. It was all lies, all of it. It had to be!

Tony turned carelessly from her. "I'm going now to have a look at my 'disabled' jeep. It doesn't really need fixing, of course. I simply removed a small, but vital, part last night. But I'll be around for a few days until your husband gets the message. Better see that he cooperates, Eleanor. That's the only way you'll get rid of me this time."

He swaggered off. Eleanor hadn't the slightest doubt that he was serious. Numbly she watched him walk down the sheep trail toward the road. She was unable to move, though the sun beat down with terrible, burning force, making her temples throb.

She couldn't seem to absorb what Tony had said. Either he was completely crazy, or he really did have some facts on which to base his accusations! Whichever it was, she had to find out. She would not be blackmailed any longer. She had paid, not in money, but emotionally, and the price had already been too high.

She walked slowly toward the laboratories.

A hot wind was blowing steadily from the desert, raising swirls of sand and dust that made the air almost unbreathable. In the makeshift pens the sheep lay with their backs to the wind.

Eleanor had never felt so desolate in her life. How would she ever get rid of Tony? She had to admit he was quite amazing. She couldn't recall that he had ever learned enough of the French language to palm himself off as a Frenchman. Still, she considered, in his line of work he had probably acquired any number of skills. He was certainly ambitious enough. . . .

With all her heart she wished she could talk to Jason now. But how could she? How could she take him away from his work, to present him with Tony's bizarre story? He was near exhaustion from overwork; it simply would not be fair.

She gave a little start as the lab door swung open. Jason stepped out, and her heart nearly burst with wild relief. She would run to him, take shelter in his arms and let him soothe her, take away the ugly impressions of Tony's face, Tony's words. . . .

Jason's face had lost its distracted expression of the past few days. He was looking directly at her now, and his eyes were blazing with anger. Eleanor stopped short in bewilderment and shock. She had never seen his anger before, not this anger. The happy exclamation that had risen to her lips abruptly died. Instead her voice shook. "Jason, wh-what . . . ?"

He strode toward her and seized her arm in a rough grip. The harsh fury in his eyes made her shrink involuntarily. "All right, Eleanor. I know you're bored. I know I haven't been able to give you any attention out here in this hellhole. But did you have to bring him here?" His low, grating voice was that of a stranger. And the words were those of a madman!

"What? *Bring* him here?"

"This Chessy, or whoever he is. I tried not to pay any attention in Damascus. One of Samir's servants saw you meet him in the bazaar. I know it was him now. I saw him watching you last night. And this morning at breakfast. But you pretended you didn't know him from Adam, didn't you?"

Eleanor faltered. In her horror at his wild assumption she could not form the right words. "Jason, I—"

"Don't try to explain. I watched your little tête-à-tête out here. You obviously know him very well indeed. All I had to do was call Hassan to the window. Jacques Chessy is the man he saw you with. You gave him money in Damascus, Eleanor. What is he, some boyfriend from the past you've never told me about?"

Eleanor stepped back as if he had struck her. "Jason, you don't understand—"

"I *do* understand. It was wrong of me to bring a wife out here. It was wrong of me to rush into marriage in the first place. What could I really know about you?" His hand gripped her arm like a steel vise, and his words battered her in a torrent of anger and pain. Each one left her weaker than the last, and each one stretched wider this new chasm that had suddenly opened between them. Still Eleanor could not speak. Her disbelief and horror paralyzed her completely.

Jason went on, his voice ragged. "And what could I have been thinking of, getting involved with a girl like you, a girl who tiptoed around behind me and turned up mysteriously uninvited in my hotel room? I trusted you then for reasons I couldn't explain even to myself: you and your big, innocent eyes, the sudden tears...who knows? But I trusted you. I accepted your 'logical' explanation. Because I wanted to. Because I thought I saw in you something different, something special.

"Then along came Samir with the strange story his servant had told him.

"I trusted you again Eleanor. I didn't bother to question you about the incident in Damascus. I thought there must be some logical explanation. Now I see. There was an explanation all right. Why didn't you tell me?"

Irrationally an answering anger rose in Eleanor. "Why didn't I tell you about my past?" Her voice quavered on the edge of tears. "Why haven't you told me about *your* past? You brought me here to live cheek by jowl with two women—two women, Jason—who are both so smitten by your fatal charm that they can't see straight for hating me. Myriam *and* Lorraine, Jason. You never told me about them!"

He drew himself up, his glacial eyes radiating sudden calm. "So that's it. You've been brooding over gossip, about things that are long dead or never were. Well, I'll tell you something. We are going to talk about this. I'm going into Damascus to do some things that can't wait. But *you* had better wait. See that Chessy keeps his hands off you until I get back!" He turned abruptly and strode away.

Eleanor seemed to feel a physical pain deep within her as she watched him go. "Jason, no! Please!" she whispered. But the sound was lost in the sighing of the desert wind.

Her world had collapsed, crushed and broken by anger and hate. She could not move. Jason ducked into the living quarters, giving the door a resounding slam. It was as if he had gone from her forever.

An eternity seemed to pass as she stood lost in desolation. Then behind her the laboratory door opened again. Paul struggled out, whistling disjointedly as he struggled with several pieces of equipment.

Eleanor watched him, her mind dulled by the emotional tides within her.

"Hey, haven't you got anything to do?" Paul joked. "Give me a hand here."

Automatically Eleanor went to him and took hold of some of the harnesses and buckets that were festooning his arms.

"Great!" declared Paul. "At least now I'm in balance. Are you all right? You look a little lost. Why don't you come up to the sheep pens with me?"

Dumbly Eleanor nodded. Paul cheerfully led the way. "Sure you're okay?" he asked again over his shoulder.

"Yes—yes, I'm fine. I was just looking for something to do, in fact. You saved my life." She tried to smile at him and brushed the wind-driven sand from her face.

"It's rotten weather to be out in," Paul shouted into the wind. "Fit only for guys like me with leather instead of skin. Maybe you should be indoors."

"No. I'd rather help you."

They trudged through the burning sand to the pens. Once inside they were able, like the sheep, to turn their backs to the wind.

"So you're not going to Damascus after all, I hear," said Paul.

"Jason didn't mention it," was all Eleanor could answer.

"Oh, sorry. Well, he said in the lab that he'd be just shooting in and out—not staying over—and that if anything would be worse for you than being here, it would be jouncing along those desert roads in the jeep."

Eleanor swallowed her feelings. There was no use going into it. She couldn't settle anything with Jason until he got back. She said nothing and busied herself helping Paul to collect and seal a blood specimen from each of the sheep. There were scores of animals, and it was a long, back-breaking morning. Eleanor was grateful for the work. It meant that she had no time to think.

By early afternoon her throat was parched, her hands black with dirt, and her eyes and hair filled with grit.

Paul straightened up from the last animal. "That's it. All labeled, too. Eleanor, I can't thank you enough—this could've taken all day. Hey, you've just about had it! Come on back to the mess hall."

Eleanor struggled back down the trail behind him, carrying a rack of samples. They took these into the lab.

Samir came toward them down the length of the big, rectangular room with its rough cinder block walls and high, barred windows, protected from the sun by inside awnings.

"You two have put in quite a morning!" he exclaimed, giving Eleanor a little bow. "Your help is very much appreciated, Mrs. Romanel." He gave directions to Myriam to refrigerate the blood samples. Then he turned again to Eleanor. "I must tell you, your husband has gone to Damascus. He wanted to tell you himself, but he saw that you were deeply involved with your work. He said to say that he wishes to be back tomorrow, and he'll see you then."

Eleanor knew she must look absolutely crestfallen. She was too tired to hide her feelings.

Samir's dark eyes lowered. Something subtle—pity . . . contempt—had passed through them.

Eleanor's cheeks burned. They must be watching her, all of them! The silly bride whose man had begun to take her for granted. . . .

Again she braced herself and looked around, meeting all their eyes: Myriam's, Claude's, Lorraine's. She held herself as proudly as her tired

muscles would permit and spoke into the awkward silence: "I know how urgent this job has
become. I only hope Jason doesn't exhaust himself
completely."

They seemed relieved and went back to their
test tubes and slides. Eleanor tried to ignore the
strange flicker she'd seen in Lorraine's wide, gray
eyes. That faraway look was for Jason, not for her
dead husband! Eleanor felt sad and obscurely
angry at the same time.

She turned to go. Paul put a protective hand on
her shoulder.

"I'll get some lunch into this lady," he told
Samir. "She's pretty worn out."

They crossed the dining hall and went out into
the afternoon heat. Eleanor's legs would barely
carry her, and she began, in spite of herself, to
tremble. Paul herded her gently inside into the
relative coolness.

"Hey," he said, "it'll be all right. He's only gone
for a day."

Eleanor sat down, leaning her chin on two
clenched fists. "I know. It's all right, really it
is."

Paul brought her a drink of fruit juice. "Here.
This'll make you feel better." He was fussing like a
mother hen, and Eleanor felt comforted by his
clumsy attentions.

Then, absurdly, those betraying tears came to
her eyes. Eleanor fought furiously, but Paul had
spotted them.

"All right, my girl. You're going to tell me

what's going on. There's more to this than meets the eye, isn't there?"

Eleanor snuffled into his proffered handkerchief. She looked for a moment at Paul with his homely, weather-beaten face and those crinkled kind eyes. She shook her head.

"Come on," he said firmly. "Let's have it. You've been bottling something up. I have a right to know what because I suspect it affects Jason's happiness. And I'm his best friend. So tell me."

"Paul, I don't know where to begin. It's all because—all because I didn't tell him about Derek in Paris."

"Derek?"

"My stepbrother. I went to Paris to see him. But he got arrested over some money, which he left in *my* room, and then his friend Tony, this petty little crook, turned up and tried to bully me—but I turned the money in—"

"Wait a moment! Slow down. What money? Start at the beginning and tell me slowly."

So Eleanor did. She told him about the Hotel Ariana, and Tony's sudden appearance, and Derek's arrest, and meeting Jason. She told him especially about the money and what Tony had said about room seventy-six and the man from Damascus. And finally she told him that Tony had accused Jason of stealing the formula from the lab above Samir's in Damascus.

Paul listened very carefully, saying nothing, only nodding now and then.

"And now Tony's blackmailing me..." Eleanor

finished. "He says he'll 'blow the whistle' to the Syrian authorities if I don't get Jason to give him two hundred thousand dollars."

Paul's eyes widened. "Wow! He's got nerve. I'll give him that," he said with a low whistle. "But how can he do it? How can he say such a thing about Jason? What *proof* has he got?"

"None. Underworld talk, that's all."

"But does he know where you are?"

"Of course! That's the worst part! Tony Belmont is Jacques Cressy...the journalist with the 'broken-down' jeep!"

Paul scowled. "I'll fix him good, the dirty creep. Blackmail—the lowest of the low. And he's approached *you* instead of Jason because you're a woman and vulnerable, I suppose. And you just might believe him."

"No! I don't! I can't believe that of Jason."

"I just thought—you married quickly, and you might be open to suggestion—that sort of thing."

"No, not that. Even though—even though Jason neglected to tell me about the women in his past, I still *trust* him...."

"Right," said Paul stoutly. "I've known him ever since university. But I wonder where Belmont's story came from? Maybe somebody *has* stolen the formula. It's certainly worth a lot of money—the research lab is a closely guarded installation, but you never know—"

"Who had access to the lab building?" Eleanor interrupted.

Paul looked thoughtful. "Well...all of us, I

suppose. Samir kept the keys, but each day of the week one of us went early to open up and was entrusted with them. . . ."

"Well then, anyone on the team could have stolen it. Anyone could be 'the connection' as Tony calls it. The man from Damascus could even be a woman!"

Paul gave her a startled look. "You think the formula really *was* stolen and sold?"

"Yes. It must have been. Where would Tony get a story like that? Why else would he go to so much trouble to get himself out here to the desert? Why is he so sure he can get all that money out of me?"

But Eleanor's excitement suddenly disappeared as one dark thought clouded her mind: anyone might have stolen the formula. But only one person was in Paris to *sell* it. And that person was Jason.

Paul noticed her sudden silence.

"Okay," he said. "The key to it all is this Tony, or Jacques, as he calls himself. I've got to find out what his information really is." He pounded a fist on the table and stood up.

"Here's what we do. Until Jason returns, string the guy along. Let him think he has you over a barrel. . .that you're going to talk to Jason, and you believe his story. We'll say nothing to anyone and do our best to get the real facts, if there *are* any."

"I've been thinking, Paul. If anybody's the man from Damascus, wouldn't it likely be Samir? Maybe he regularly smuggles things out. You said yourself he didn't earn all that money being Dr. Marouk."

"That's true. I'm not sure where his money comes from. I assumed it was 'family' because he wields such authority, like a noble of some kind. I'm not really up on Arab customs."

"I'm only saying it because he seems so... closed, somehow sinister. There's something about him I don't trust."

"Woman's intuition, huh? Samir *is* rather reserved, I'll grant you that. Perhaps he's a legitimate avenue of inquiry." Paul took Eleanor firmly by the shoulders. "But don't do it yourself, hear? I'm going to settle with this creep Tony for you. You just watch your step and play dumb. And don't go around playing detective, okay? If Samir, or anybody else here is involved with this so-called million-dollar deal, he or she could be very dangerous."

"Paul, there's just one thing...."

"What's that?"

"What if it *is* Jason?"

"Well then, you'd want to know, wouldn't you?"

Eleanor felt her stomach tighten. "Yes...I suppose I would," she said very quietly.

ELEANOR AVOIDED the supper group that night. She knew she ought to present a cheerful face, let them know she was "pulling" with the team. But she couldn't bear the thought of Tony's sardonic double entendres, as he masqueraded, playing

"Jacques Chessy" to the hilt. And the suspicions that tumbled about in her mind as she lay awake in the strangely empty bed grew more and more confusing.

In the morning Saoud, the cook, brought her tea. She felt as though she hadn't slept at all. She sipped the strong, hot tea thoughtfully, reviewing the events of the day before.

She was feeling less isolated, at least. Myriam and Lorraine, she presumed, still eyed her with reserve and envy. And Claude was buried deep in his work.

And Samir: those eyes—their liquid, obsidian gaze was inescapable. He seemed to watch her, to watch them all. But he was unreadable.

But the sense of isolation was truly relieved only by Paul. Thank heaven for him! She felt at least a little protected from Tony, and surely Paul would help her answer all the terrible questions he had raised.

Eleanor shuddered inwardly. She must get up and continue to do what she could to help the team.

They worked steadily all day. Tony hung around, taking notes and photos, seemingly enjoying his role as a visiting journalist. Eleanor tried to ignore his sly glances, keeping herself very busy. Paul gave her a reassuring grin every chance he got.

By suppertime Eleanor was too tired and hungry to worry about Tony's surveillance in the mess hall. She ate with the group and was having her usual tea instead of the coffee everyone else drank before he spoke directly to her.

"I see your husband hasn't returned, Mrs. Romanel." To everyone but Eleanor the remark sounded perfectly sincere—a routine, even sympathetic inquiry.

"He has a lot to do in Damascus," Eleanor replied evenly. "He'll probably be back tomorrow."

Samir broke in. "Yes. It must have simply taken extra time for him to analyze the test results."

Eleanor sensed their eyes on her. She could not muster more than a nod. Paul changed the subject, and she shot him a grateful glance.

After dinner Paul took her aside. "Not much to report. I've been doing some roundabout chatting with Claude. It won't do to talk openly in case Belmont gets wind of it of course. Right now I don't know whether we can eliminate Samir from suspicion or not. Now don't worry. Just carry on. You're doing fine."

"I'm worried, Paul. I can't help it. What if Tony gets the wrong idea about Jason's not coming back? What if he thinks Jason is getting out of his reach?"

"He won't. You're here, aren't you? Anyway, Jason'll be back tomorrow." he reassured her.

Yes, I'm here, Eleanor thought. *But that doesn't mean a thing to Jason.*

Later, as she crawled wearily into bed, she said a silent, fervent prayer. *Let him come back. He must come back tomorrow!*

She had to speak to him and explain everything—as she should have done from the first. If only he would listen! Why, oh, why had she blurted out those things about Myriam and Lorraine?

Eleanor was suddenly aware of her terrible loneliness. Jason was gone, and he had been her home, her strength, throughout these long days in the searing caldron of the desert; he was her friend, her lover, her husband and companion. Even though he had been working for long exhausting hours, the knowledge of his presence, the need to help him if she could, had been the focus of Eleanor's life. Now, there were only this group of strangers and the predator, Tony Belmont.

But there was Paul, she reminded herself. He was her only ally, the only one she could trust. But what could Paul do? He was well-meaning, but clumsy—a sort of overgrown boy scout. Still, he was all she had.

Eleanor fell into a troubled sleep.

She awoke early the next day, feeling ill. She was violently sick to her stomach and felt strangely dizzy. She examined the dark circles under her eyes, using Jason's little shaving mirror. The paleness of her cheeks made the smudges even more stark. Having thrown up, she began to feel gradually better. She decided she must have eaten something slightly "off" the previous night.

The day dragged by with no sign of Jason. There was no word from him, either. Paul was constantly reassuring. "Look, he's probably absolutely desperate because he can't phone us here at camp, but I'll bet he'll send a message. He'll be here as soon as he can, probably tomorrow. I know he will."

That night as Eleanor headed for her quarters, Tony intercepted her.

"What's happening?" he hissed, his face shadowy in the light from her flashlight.

"I told you: he's got a lot to do. He'll be back as soon as he can. Don't bother me—I've got a headache."

Tony chuckled. It was an ugly sound. "Well, I hope your precious husband knows what'll happen to you if he doesn't come back."

Eleanor glared at Tony, but said nothing. Instead, she slammed the door in his face, glad of any opportunity to be rude to him.

The next morning she experienced the same nausea and dizziness she had suffered the day before. Again she was sick to her stomach. She ate nothing at breakfast because the sight of food brought new waves of nausea over her.

At noon with the blistering sun high overhead everything began to spin so violently around her that she had to lean against the fence of the sheep pen.

"Are you all right?" Paul's voice was far away. A strange, yellow mist seemed to envelop her, and the world tilted suddenly away. . . .

"I CARRIED YOU IN out of the sun," Paul said when she opened her eyes. "You fainted, girl. Say, you know, you look lousy. You're pale as a ghost. And those eyes—they're like a panda bear's."

"I was a little sick this morning—didn't eat," said Eleanor weakly.

"I'll get Samir to look at you. Hang on!"

"No, no, it's all right really—"

But he was gone. A few minutes later, Samir came in.

"I've noticed...you're not looking well, Mrs. Romanel." He touched her pulse and forehead. "Any pains?"

"Just a headache. I'm sure it's nothing."

"Still, you had better rest for the afternoon." Silently Samir went out and closed the door.

Eleanor dozed fitfully in the relative coolness of the sleeping quarters. Time reeled by in a strange kaleidoscope of dreams. The images seemed to merge with reality: Tony, smiling his evil smile; Paul, looking down at her, concern etched on his face; Jason....

Once in the dimness someone came into the room and inserted a needle into Eleanor's arm. Was it real or a dream? She tried to open her eyes, to see the person's face. But heaviness weighed her limbs, and her mind slipped down again, down into its dreams....

She heard voices, sometimes hushed, sometimes abnormally loud.

"We'll have to get Dr. Khaddad from Hama," said one.

"Here, try her on this hot tea," said another.

"Do you suppose it's pregnancy, complicated perhaps by the heat and these horrible conditions?" That voice was a woman's, but it faded, blending into the rest. Eleanor sensed that the room was first light, then dark. Were hours or days passing? She couldn't tell, nor did she care.

Then at last she awoke with a clear head. The room was empty. She realized that she had been very ill, for she felt weak. She couldn't have eaten or drunk anything for many hours . . . or was it days? Her head felt very light, but she was able to totter over to the window and look out. It was daytime now.

She tried to sort out her confused memories but her brain refused to cooperate. The strange images and impressions reeled, leaving her with only questions. How long had she been ill? Where was Jason? Had he been here, or had she only dreamed that he had? Who was the woman—yes, it had been a woman—in the night with a hypodermic, she wondered.

Eleanor had an urgent need to find out what had been going on. She fumbled about and located some clothing. By the time she was dressed, the dizzy feeling had lessened; she definitely needed something to eat, something very light, perhaps some soup. Yes, that would make her feel stronger. She would make her way to the kitchen first, then go to the lab and find out whatever she could. Everyone must be working.

Unsteadily she walked to the mess hall. The entire building seemed to be deserted. The place seemed unearthly still, breathlessly silent in the desert afternoon.

Saoud was not in the kitchen. She would have

to find something for herself in the pantry. Her hands trembled as she tried to open the storage-room door.

Eleanor frowned. The door was stubbornly closed, stuck somehow. The latch opened freely, but the door itself would not. Something seemed to be blocking it. Eleanor pushed as hard as she could, but the door only gave an inch or two. It was as if there was a deadweight of some kind behind it.

A cold sweat broke out on Eleanor's forehead. She let out a little cry of frustration. Oh, why wouldn't the thing open? All she wanted was a cup of tea, or a slice of bread. But it was too much for her. She would have to get someone to help her. . . .

"Hey! What're you doing up and running about?" someone yelled.

Paul's voice, thank heaven! She turned and gave him a wan smile of gratitude as he strode toward her through the kitchen.

"Paul! You've saved my life again! I just want some tea or something, but I can't get into the pantry for some reason. The door seems to be stuck, or else I'm impossibly weak. . . ."

"Why didn't you come and get me before? Luckily I just went to check on you and found you gone—so I instituted a little search. You've had us worried, you know."

"I'm better, honestly. If I could get something light in my stomach, I know I'd be practically one hundred percent."

"Well then, we'd better get this door open, hadn't we? What seems to be wrong?" he asked gently.

"Don't know." Eleanor's teeth chattered feverishly. "There's something heavy behind the door. Maybe some flour sacks fell over."

"Let me try. There. One good shove and—" His words were abruptly cut off. "Wait, Eleanor. Don't look."

"What is it?" Paul put out an arm to stop her, but Eleanor ducked under it. She looked into the pantry through the one-foot opening Paul had forced.

Her eyes widened with shock and terror as she stared down at the obstruction that had held the door shut.

She was looking into Lorraine's eyes. They were wide and still and very empty.

Lorraine was dead.

Chapter 10

The entire team had gathered in the dining hall. There was a pall of horrified disbelief in the air. No one was able to say very much.

A note had been found along with the body. Samir glanced at it briefly and raised his eyes to the circle of stricken faces. "This is sad, very sad," he said. "I think it is a matter of some privacy, this note. I think only one person here should read it and only if she so desires."

He turned to Eleanor. "This concerns you. But perhaps you do not feel strong enough. . . ."

"I'm all right," Eleanor said. "Please let me read it if it concerns me, as you say."

"There you are then." Samir spoke to the group at large. "I'm afraid Mrs. Gray has. . .killed herself."

There were murmurs of dismay and anguish.

Samir continued. "I suggest we disperse. I must

arrange the proper procedures. We must get the police from Hama. Saoud, please give Mrs. Romanel some broth. I think she is very weak."

Samir continued to give instructions, but Eleanor did not hear the rest. She sat frozen in her chair, reading the pathetic note. It was typewritten, except for the signature, and in English.

Dear Eleanor Romanel,
    Yes, that is your name. But it is I who should be Mrs. Romanel. Have I not done everything for him? But this last thing I cannot possibly continue. I have drunk the same bitter brew with which I tried to poison you. I think that you may live, but I must die. I put arsenic trioxide into the tea, knowing you to be the only one who uses it. I wanted to make you sick so you would leave. But I cannot continue. Now he is gone; what he planned for us is gone. I know all about it, what he did, but the secret dies with me.
                    Lorraine

Eleanor read the note through twice, then a third time. Poison? Lorraine had tried to poison her! Had Jason instructed Lorraine to poison her? But that was incredible! Yet the note specifically said: "Have I not done everything for him? But this last thing I cannot possibly continue." And the "secret" that had died with her—it could only mean one thing—the stolen formula. Eleanor was shocked.... So Jason _had_ done all the things

Tony had accused him of! He had some kind of hold over Lorraine, a much stronger one than Paul had implied when he told Eleanor that Lorraine and Jason had once been a little more than good friends. Thunderstruck, Eleanor tried to fit the pieces together. Not only was someone dead, but that same someone had tried to *kill* her. And what was worse—what was impossible, but true—was that Jason had been involved!

She heard again Tony's terrible accusations—that Jason was the connection in Damascus, the mastermind of a plot to steal the million-dollar fuel formula. Why would he want his wife out of the way suddenly? Eleanor couldn't believe it was because of his irrational jealousy over her meetings with Tony.... She became acutely conscious of the irony in the situation: the terrible, sickening irony. The impossible had happened, and the despicable Tony had been right all along.

Her heart seemed to crumple within her. All the strength was gone from her body, and she began to tremble uncontrollably. She felt someone slip a jacket over her shoulders.

Paul, again. He took the note from her limp fingers. "Poison!" he exclaimed after a moment. "She tried to poison you? Whatever for?"

Eleanor looked around the room. She and Paul were alone. No one could hear. "We must keep that note from the police," she said, her voice dull but precise. "Samir didn't read it carefully. He *can't* know what it says, what it means. He thinks Lorraine tried to poison me out of jealousy."

"Well, didn't she?" Paul asked.

"Don't you see what it says? *Jason* wanted me poisoned!"

"Now you're crazy!"

" ..And he did it—he stole the formula, just as Tony said. I suppose they were in it together until I turned up. It's so funny—I believed in him so much, was so proud of his work...but it was all a sham, used to fool the Syrians, to take advantage of a position of trust. I can't believe it yet, can't understand it...." Her voice trailed off.

Paul knelt down beside her chair, his face mirroring bewilderment and distress. Eleanor remembered Paul's loyalty to Jason, their long and rich friendship, and realized he, too, must feel betrayed. His voice was gentle though when he spoke. "Look, the note doesn't say those things, not in so many words. She could have meant anything."

"Don't you *see* it, Paul," Eleanor cried. "It doesn't have to say any more. We *know*. You did say the thief was dangerous. But Lorraine was weak. She couldn't go through with it. It's all there. And I remember now, she came into my room with a hypodermic when I was so ill. I was only half-conscious and couldn't fight her. She stuck it into my arm. Probably an extra dose...."

Paul rubbed his temples. "No...it doesn't make sense, Eleanor. Why would Jason want you dead?"

"Because he knew somehow that I knew about the formula. I don't know how—unless Tony approached him after all...but that couldn't be. He had the crazy idea that Tony was my lover. He saw me talking to him after I had pretended not to know him. And some spy of Samir's saw me with Tony in Damascus. He reported it to Jason. I don't know how he knew—but he must have. He wouldn't kill me just out of jealousy—"

"I can't believe it...it just doesn't make sense," Paul interjected.

"It does make sense. How many days have I been sick?"

"Three."

"And Jason is *still* not back from Damascus, right? Did you expect him to take so long? Did anyone?" demanded Eleanor.

Paul shook his head and watched her uncertainly.

"He has sent no letters, no telegrams. He's not *coming* back, Paul, don't you understand?" she cried.

Paul was still speechless. He studied the note as if it was some sort of hieroglyph...some code that he could unlock, if only he knew how, that would reveal the truth. His brow creased deeply.

Eleanor was silent for a long moment, and then she spoke slowly, dreamily. "Tony was right about him. Lorraine knew his secret, too. Somehow he knew he'd be found out, and he's made his escape."

Eleanor's shoulders sagged as if physically burdened by the revelations in the suicide note.

"There may be reasons why he's not back," Paul said without conviction.

"There can be no reason for his not contacting us. No other reason except his need to escape."

"Jason *did* steal the formula?" Paul's words trailed off as if he was unwilling to believe them.

Eleanor roused herself. "We have to get rid of that note, Paul. They can't suspect."

"But that's criminal!" he protested.

"I don't care. I won't be the one to turn Jason in to the authorities." Her physical energy had returned. She stood up and squared her shoulders. "We'll type a new note, Paul. One that explains only that Lorraine was jealous. Come on to the lab."

Paul looked uncertain, but she refused to be deterred, and he strode after her helplessly. Once in the lab where they were alone Eleanor retyped the note on all-purpose paper identical to that used for the original note. The typewriter was even the same as the one Lorraine had employed. She left out all the references to Jason's "secret" and the hint that Lorraine had done the poisoning at his instructions.

"What about the signature?" Paul asked hesitantly.

"Trace it. Can you try?" she asked, feeling strangely calm.

Clumsily Paul made a few practice attempts. "No use, Eleanor. I'm too ham-handed."

Eleanor took the pen and tried. The result wasn't perfect, but she decided it would have to do. "Now the authorities will have no reason to investigate Jason," she announced, tearing up the old note. "We'll burn this!"

"Eleanor, aren't you confused? You decided Jason wasn't coming back, remember?"

"He could come back. He might, you know. Or they might go after him."

"But—what are you going to do?" Paul asked, wide-eyed.

"I'm taking the first boat, train, or plane back to Canada. I can't be here if Jason does turn up. I don't trust myself because I still love him. In spite of everything." She looked helplessly at Paul.

He bent his shaggy head and scuffed a toe. "Okay, I'll help you if you like...if that's what you want."

"Paul, it's the only way. I'll turn our new note over to Samir for the inquest, or whatever. And then I've got to go."

"But there's one fly in the ointment, you know." Paul stared at her with solemn eyes. She returned the look, knowing what he meant. Tony Belmont. Tony would continue to hound her and hound Jason if he could.

"What'll we do about him?" Paul asked.

"Let's turn him over to the police. He's here on forged papers after all."

"You can't do that, Eleanor. He might 'blow the whistle' on Jason, and that's just what you don't want—"

"That's why I hope Jason *is* gone," Eleanor put in.

"But Tony will follow you, thinking Jason will contact you. You *are* his wife."

Eleanor sighed bitterly. "I can't think why he did that—married me, I mean. Right in the middle of his big coup. But why *would* he try to reach me? He has all he wants. If he'd wanted me, he wouldn't have gone without me. No, Jason wants me out of the way now. He wants it badly enough to have had Lorraine try to poison me...." Eleanor's brain rebelled at this thought, the image of Jason trying to kill her by proxy. She could picture only the bleakness of her life from now on without him.

But she shrugged these thoughts away. She must not look back, not yet. She had to get away, shake Tony off her trail. It was becoming a familiar scenario. "Tony...yes...what'll I do about him?"

Paul scowled. "Well, I won't have him hanging around you forever. Let me think. There must be something we can do.. ." Paul paced back and forth with long-legged strides, his shoulders hunched in concentration. "Where is he now, I wonder?" he asked at length.

"With the others, probably. Working on his 'journalist' pose—though suicides aren't news. Poor Lorraine."

"Poor Lorraine! She tried to *kill* you!"

"I can't help it. I understand her a little, I guess."

"Good Lord! Women! Oh, I don't understand, not really. And I'm not happy about whatever it is she says Jason has done. But I'm more than willing to do one thing—and that's help you to get rid of that rotten little blackmail artist." He paced some more. "Now, look. I've got a plan, I think. First, we've got to get him away from camp, lure him to Hama. It's the nearest town. I want him away from here, and I want to see what I can arrange with some of the locals."

"Like what, Paul?"

"I'm going to see if I can get a couple of Arab fellows to sort of incapacitate him just for a few days until you get away."

"It's so... grubby—"

"Not if you don't want to involve the police! Eleanor, we have to.. "

Silently Eleanor acquiesced.

The plan was laid. There were still several hours of daylight. Eleanor and Paul would go to Hama on the pretext of seeing a doctor there.

Tony would receive a very broad hint that Eleanor was flying the coop and might be expected to try to follow them. He couldn't physically stop Eleanor, not while she had Paul to protect her. But Paul would make sure that Tony saw him put Eleanor's suitcases into the truck.

It was not an entirely reliable plan, but it was born of desperation—and it just might work, they had decided.

Next they sought out Samir. Had the police been fetched from Hama yet, Paul wanted to know. Dully Samir replied they hadn't.

"In that case," announced Paul, "I'll take care of it. We're going into town so that Eleanor can be checked for serious consequences—if there are any—of the attempted poisoning."

Samir agreed. Both Eleanor and Paul watched Tony as he covertly listened in on this conversation.

Eleanor hurried to the sleeping quarters. Paul drew the truck up in front of the door and a short time later got out to help Eleanor into the passenger seat. He placed her bags in the back with a loud thump, waiting a minute or two before climbing into the driver's seat.

They drove out of camp and took the turn toward Hama. They had been on the road for only a few minutes when Paul looked into the rearview mirror and smiled grimly. "See that cloud of dust? What do you want to bet that's our Tony?"

Elanor looked over her shoulder. There was a jeep on the road, all right. "Don't let him lose us," she said.

"Don't worry about that!" Paul drove skillfully, and Eleanor was silent, fighting off the surges of pain and regret that threatened to overwhelm her. Every mile they drove was taking her further away from Jason.

Don't look back, cried an inner voice. *Not yet. You'll have years ahead for regrets....*

They raced along the highway at top speed, always keeping the jeep in sight, until finally the mosques and buildings of Hama came into view. Paul drove the truck into the town's main square and parked.

Tony's vehicle was no longer behind them; it

had slipped back in the columns of traffic. Paul seemed to consider for a moment. "You sit here," he said, "in the truck. I won't be gone for more than a minute or two. And if he gets to the square, he'll see you right away. He'll know he hasn't lost us. I don't think he'll try to do anything at this point. . . he'll just be wanting to keep tabs on us— to see what we're going to do next. I'll get a couple of sturdy men, and we'll spring the trap. He won't know what hit him until a couple of days from now—and you'll be safely away by then on a flight to Canada. All right? Not nervous, are you?"

"No," said Eleanor. "Tony gives me the creeps, but despite his dire threats I'm not afraid of him. I'll just sit here nonchalantly and let him think I haven't got the slightest idea he's watching."

"Okay, then," Paul said, and he jumped out of the vehicle and loped across the square. There were hundreds of people about, and Eleanor could easily keep track of Paul's progress because of his height. He ducked into an alleyway that wound off into a maze of sunbaked buildings.

She looked cautiously around the square, checking for signs of Tony or his jeep. She still couldn't see it. Perhaps he hadn't taken the bait after all! She began to fidget. Just sitting in the hot cab of the truck made her increasingly edgy. There must be something more practical she could do. She decided to get out—to find some shade and watch the truck from a distance. If Tony spotted it empty, he might show himself.

Since they hadn't made any progress in drawing him closer into their snare her new idea seemed like the best cause. Eleanor eagerly stretching her tired legs.

She walked boldly across the square in the opposite direction from that which Paul had taken. She looked neither to the left nor the right until she had reached a row of shop fronts, protected by awnings. For a moment or two she gazed at the goods on display, then turned very casually to face the square again. She scanned the crowd carefully. There were water sellers and fruit peddlers...men in fatigues and suits, women veiled and not veiled.... Brown-skinned street urchins darted in and out.

Traffic hooted, jingled and even brayed, if it happened to be the four-footed variety. People of every description passed to and fro, but there was no sign of Tony Belmont.

Eleanor sighed. Perhaps he was cleverer than they had given him credit for being. If the plan Paul had worked out failed, Eleanor knew she would be at a loss, doomed to the same hunted feeling that had accompanied her days ever since Paris...that had given her nightmares and unhappy daytime fantasies.

Tony, you'd better show up! She clenched her jaw in anger as her restless eyes scanned the square.

Suddenly Eleanor's scalp tingled. She saw him!

He was strolling along the street with his hands deep in his pockets, wearing dark glasses and looking casually about. His camera was flung around his neck, and anyone but Eleanor would have mistaken him for a rubbernecking tourist. He came abreast of the truck and went by it without pausing.

How could he miss it? Eleanor felt her nails digging into her palms. But wait! Tony stopped with his back to her and aimed his camera at something in the square. Then he looked sideways at the truck. They hadn't been mistaken! He had risen to their bait. But where was Paul?

Eleanor drew deeper into the shaded doorway of the shop. She mustn't let Tony see her yet—not until she knew what Paul was up to.

But where was he? Her impatience was making her heart pound painfully, and she felt the first signs of a returning headache.

Then Tony began to walk away. Eleanor's stomach twisted. She must keep him in sight until Paul returned! She began to follow him.

The jostling crowd made her task a difficult one. She could barely concentrate on a man walking thirty yards ahead of her when she had to pay constant attention to the people immediately in front of her. She kept losing sight of Tony, but she hurried on, trying now to close the gap between them. It was risky, she knew, but there was no alternative.

She was practically walking on tiptoe, trying to spot him. Without warning the crowd parted just ahead of her, and Tony was hurtling toward her.

There was a strange look on his face behind the

elaborate sunglasses. His mouth was open in a rictus of surprise or shock. Eleanor was herself so surprised that she stopped in her tracks, staring at the scrambling figure of Tony. He was only a few feet from her when he pitched forward and landed face down in a grotesque sprawl.

With a sense of jarring terror Eleanor stared down at him. His head was twisted to one side, and the sunglasses, broken, lay beside him.

Blood spurted from his nose and mouth. His eyes stared fixedly at nothing at all.

The smothering crowd seemed to seesaw back and forth, to swim in and out of Eleanor's perception. She was unable for a moment to grasp what this meant, this horror at her feet. She only knew that she had seen something very like it before... in fact, not long ago at all. Had it been this morning? Yes...a photographic image of Lorraine's eyes, wide and staring in death, snapped into her brain.

Eleanor raised a fist to her mouth, trying to stifle a scream.

The crowd shoved and pushed her, elbowing toward the still, crumpled man. Eleanor was pushed aside, but she could barely feel what was happening, could barely hear or see....

Then Paul was there, taking her arm firmly and walking her zombie body away from all the people. The smells, colors and noises of the marketplace were rocketing around her, a meaningless swirl. She forgot for a moment where she was, who she was with. She was being hurried along, past staring people. She heard from far away Paul's voice.

"That does it, dammit! There are bound to be questions. Got to get you away. . . ."

But Eleanor did not understand. What was he talking about? The death? Tony's death. He *was* dead—suddenly she was sure of that. Paul steered her along quickly now. Shocked, she went without protest.

They ducked into a maze of alleyways. As the dimness closed over them, Eleanor heard a scuffle of running feet behind them.

Paul jerked his head around. "Already?" he gasped. "Hurry, run."

His grip on her arm was iron, inescapable. He pulled urgently, and Eleanor stumbled along obediently as fast as she could.

"This way," Paul ordered. They turned sharply to the left, then to the right, diving between hanging rugs into the sudden darkness of a shop.

Where were they? What had they done? Tony Belmont. . .dead? That wasn't the plan. Eleanor could make no sense of the crazy images, the echoing words that spun in her head. And now they were hidden in this eerie, black, stifling place. . .with oriental rugs piled everywhere in the shadows, dark and heavy as shrouds. She longed for the sunlight again, for some kind of light with which to see Paul, who was beside her, still clutching her tightly.

She tried to speak, but he slammed his palm over her mouth. "Be quiet!" he commanded in a sharp undertone. She could hear them again, the running feet. They were coming closer. There must be several people chasing them. Eleanor fought for breath. . . .

"Quick," breathed Paul, "the back way—more alleys. . . ."

Eleanor heard whistles and shouts outside. Police?

Suddenly the rugs were thrust aside, and sharp sunlight pierced the interior of the stall. Blinded, Eleanor could make out only the dark silhouettes of three men, tall against the burning afternoon outside.

Then she saw the dull gleam of metal: the men had guns. The guns were leveled at them, at her and Paul. His hand was still tight over her mouth; she squirmed, trying to get free, trying to tell him that he'd better explain everything, that the men would understand.

But Paul did a very strange thing. He wrenched her hard, trapping her even more thoroughly, and with his free hand be brought something against her throat. It was cool and metallic against her skin. . . .

"If you take one more step," panted Paul, "I'll kill her."

Eleanor was jolted by the words. She twisted frantically around, trying to see his face. What was happening to her? What was happening to Paul?

The three men seemed to be paralyzed by Paul's threat. They had stopped in their tracks. There was a dizzy moment of suspension when time stood still. Eleanor could barely breathe, still less think. She couldn't make out the features of these shadowy armed men, much less read the expressions on their faces. . . .

Then one of them spoke. "I don't think you'll do that, Paul," he said in a voice that was very hard and very precise. It was a familiar voice.

Jason!

"Why don't you just let her go, Paul?" he continued, his words deadly calm.

There was a catch in Paul's ragged, panicky breathing. The cold blade at her throat bit very slightly. It stung her. . . .

"Out of my way, Jason. You can't stop me now. How'd you get here, anyway?"

"I made it to camp just as you were pulling out. They just had time to tell me Lorraine was dead, and you'd taken my wife. They didn't know what I knew, Paul. That you had *killed* Lorraine. I knew you'd tried to kill Eleanor because Lorraine phoned me in Damascus. She ran a blood test and found the poison."

Eleanor listened, horrified. *Paul* was a killer!

"I had to kill her. I knew she'd done the test," Paul said, his voice hoarse and rasping. "But how the hell did she phone you?"

"She came all the way into Hama in the middle of the night. She'd seen you doctoring the tea, Paul."

"I've killed two now, Jason. One more won't

matter. So call off those cops and let me through if you want to see Eleanor alive again."

"Paul, you're nuts. You'll never get away."

"Why not? I've got a hostage, haven't I? And believe me, this knife is sharp. You'd better move!"

Eleanor felt Paul's grip on her relax ever so slightly as he talked. Jason was distracting him. She knew with sudden, desperate clarity that she must make a move now, or Jason would be forced to back down. No one would shoot at Paul while he shielded his body with her own. Eleanor summoned all her strength, suddenly twisting her shoulders to jam an elbow into Paul's stomach and kicking at his shin as hard as she could.

It was not totally effective, but it startled him. Before he could press the knife to her throat more tightly, he was grabbed and jerked from behind. His arms were torn from around Eleanor, and she was flung clear.

Straining in terror, she could see the knife's cold gleam as two men locked themselves in a struggle over it. The fight was brief, for the men with the guns stepped in.

Jason scooped Eleanor up in his arms and swung her out of the smothering darkness of the rug shop. In the sunlight outside he held her for a long moment. She could feel his heart pounding against her, as he silently stilled her trembling. "Okay?" he whispered, setting her on her feet.

The world, which had turned upside down for

Eleanor this morning, suddenly righted itself again as she stared wordlessly into his eyes.

Oblivious to the cursing and the struggle within the rug shop, Eleanor couldn't think, couldn't answer the questions that whirled in her mind. She could only feel the warm, solid strength of Jason's arms.

Then the struggle in the shop quieted. Two men emerged with Paul handcuffed between them. Paul glared at Jason and Eleanor as they clung together. Eleanor moved closer to Jason.

She struggled to understand. The men holding Paul were uniformed policemen. *Paul had murdered Lorraine.* But why?

Jason stared at his best friend, his eyes glacial. "Paul," he said in a strange, distant voice.

Paul's face contorted in a caricature of his old, crooked grin. "Ask Eleanor," he said in a sardonic tone. "She knows. She had it all figured out except for the villain. She got that wrong. She thought the villain was *you*, Jason—of all people. By the longest coincidence in the world you met a girl who went to Paris to meet someone with whom I was doing business. The odds against it were astronomical. But you married that girl, and you brought her here. And she figured it out."

"Why did you want to kill her, Paul?"

"I didn't really. I wanted to make her sick, to get her to go away. But I happened to catch Lorraine making tests for poison. I decided to lay the blame for the poisoning on Lorraine and get rid of her at the same time. And the ultimate blame would fall on you, Jason. Sorry about that."

"What was so important? What could make you kill, Paul? I've known you for fifteen years, and I just can't believe it—"

"It was worth millions—maybe billions. The formula, Jason, you dope. The fuel formula. *You* carried it to Paris. In your luggage. But you didn't know that. I had someone steal it. . . ."

"That was me, I'm afraid," said a new voice. Eleanor turned, startled. He had just emerged from the rug shop and stood, looking apologetically at Eleanor.

"Derek. . ." she started, but the words did not come after that.

Jason gave her a squeeze. "I know you've had enough shocks for one day, Eleanor. But your stepbrother has explained a great many things to me. He came to Syria to try to stop this Tony fellow from harming you. . . ."

"It was the least I could do," Derek said. "I'd gotten you into a mess, Eleanor."

She was still speechless. Jason held up one hand. "We can go over this later. I think we should get Eleanor out of here. She's probably at the end of her rope."

Eleanor gave him a grateful little smile. She held out a hand to Derek, and together they escorted her through the narrow streets and alleys to the Hama city square. Behind, the two Syrian policemen had Paul in a tight grip. Eleanor could not look back. She heard him curse angrily once or twice, but his monstrous betrayal of herself, of Jason, of Samir and the whole team was sinking in; her sense of revulsion would not permit her now—or perhaps ever—to look at his face. So she gazed resolutely ahead when he was led away.

Jason stared after Paul and the policemen. On his face was a look that resembled grief, but he said nothing.

BACK AT THE DESERT CAMP Jason saw to it that Eleanor slept undisturbed for over ten hours. He would permit no one to question her, or to fuss over her. "We'll talk tomorrow," he said firmly. And that was that.

Eleanor's tired brain whirled briefly with the strange events of the day, but mercifully sleep washed gently over her before she could begin to sort everything out.

The next day began with a fierce glow of sun on the eastern horizon. The sky was bathed in flamingo and gold, shading to delicate coral pink. Eleanor awoke very early. Jason had slept beside her, cradling her without a word and soothing her to sleep. She had been content last night to ask no questions, but now they crowded in on her. She waited impatiently for him to wake. There was so much she didn't understand—so much she must know.

He looked so peaceful, though, back here where he belonged, his black hair crisp against the pillowcase. She could not bring herself to disturb him. Instead she stared out at the bedouin tents, huddled on the plain and surrounded by the still sleeping sheep. The world was serene and very quiet. It was almost impossible to believe the horrors of the previous day: the discovery of Lorraine's body; the violent death of Tony. Had Paul killed him, too? It was probably true; Tony was an even greater threat to Paul's plans than Eleanor had been. He knew far too much. Paul must have decided to eliminate him under cover of trying to "help" Eleanor escape from him.

It was all unbelievably ruthless. .but then, there were millions of dollars involved. Paul had given in to greed, and it had taken him over completely—destroying all the old decency that must have been in his character for Jason to have been such a good friend to him.

Eleanor didn't know what made her the most upset: the cold-blooded murder of Lorraine, or the betrayal of Jason's friendship; or the way in which Paul had used and deceived her, allowing her to trust him, to tell him everything so that he might use all of it against her and against Jason.

On the other hand she could not get greatly upset about Tony's brutal end. Shocking it had certainly been; and no one should be condemned out of hand without trial to such a summary execution. Eleanor would not have planned for things to end like this, but Tony had put himself in harm's way by undertaking the dangerous game of blackmail in the first place. She winced, remembering the stark horror of Tony's staring eyes and all the blood on his face. . . .

"Darling, don't brood..." said Jason. He was awake and propped up on one elbow. She turned to him, and a small cry of distress escaped from her lips. Then he was holding her very gently and surely. She knew that the worst terror of all—her suspicion of Jason—was over, and that was what really mattered. The other things would fade with time. But this one thing, this precious love, was intact.

Jason's voice was husky when he spoke at last. "I can't tell you the agonies I've been through after leaving you the way I did. I wanted to come right back to you, to say that whatever this man was to you, it didn't matter, that we'd work it out...."

Eleanor tried to speak, but he laid his forefinger over her lips.

"But I was delayed a day longer than I intended because the tests I was doing were bringing some important results—I was really getting somewhere. It was our first break in all those weeks of work. So I didn't return immediately. It was a lucky thing I didn't as it turned out, but I was getting pretty agitated when two days turned into three. I knew you must be stewing out here all alone; but I couldn't telephone.

"However, I received a mysterious telephone call from Paris, France. It was from Derek. He had been searching for you for weeks ever since the incident at the Hotel Ariana. No, he wasn't in jail. The police had him on an old warrant of some kind, and the magistrate apparently rejected their evidence. He can tell you more about that.

"At any rate you can imagine my surprise at hearing from him. But his message was urgent. He knew this Tony Belmont fellow had followed you to Syria and would stop at nothing to get some money he thought you had. Derek persuaded me to wait in Damascus for him and arranged to get a flight right away. When he got to Syria, and I talked to him for a while, I began to put things together. Your reticence about your family and your past were explained. The 'lover' I had so cruelly assumed Belmont to be was explained. Derek said we should lose no time getting to you and eliminating the blackmail threat we now knew was hanging over you.

"Then I received that call from Lorraine in the middle of the night. We had to wait for morning to gas up the jeep before we could take off.

"I don't think the distance from Damascus to camp could have been covered in less time, but when we got here, we were told you'd gone off with Paul. I knew Lorraine had seen him putting poison in your tea. And Tony had taken off, too. It was quite a procession, roaring along the road to Hama.

"One nearly fatal thing happened, though. We followed Tony's jeep into town and lost sight of the truck for a while. I was beside myself.

"When Tony parked and began walking, I decided to pull around to the local police station. We needed all the help we could get."

He paused, running his fingers gently down Eleanor's cheek. "I didn't know where you were, but we had spotted the truck in the square. We headed in that direction with the police in tow. Then we saw Paul. He was just ahead of us, and there was some kind of scramble going on. I saw him with Tony. They seemed to fight, then Tony ran or stumbled through the crowd out of sight. Paul was after him, and I caught just a glimpse of that knife of his. Seconds later we came upon Tony, sprawled on the pavement. Sure enough, he had been stabbed. And we could see Paul moving away though the crowd. We left a policeman with the body and fairly flew after him.

"I was horrified to see that he had you with him. He ducked into the maze of alleys, and we gave immediate chase, but lost him for a minute or two. We got to the rug shop, though, and realized it was the only place he could have hidden in the short time he'd been out of our sight.

"And Derek went quietly around to see if there was a back entrance."

"A good thing he did," murmured Eleanor.

"Yes. But you did your own bit to break the stranglehold Paul had on you." Jason's crystal eyes kindled with warmth at the memory. "I'll have to remember how tough you can be."

Eleanor was bemused. The idea of Derek being a hero and helping to save her was something new and surprising. "I had given up on Derek," she murmured.

"Well, he has redeemed himself somewhat, you've got to admit. Even if he did break into my room at the Hotel Ariana and steal a piece of paper from my luggage. It was written in code, you know, and made to look like perfectly ordinary correspondence. He only knew he was getting twenty thousand for making off with it."

"Oh, dear. The money . . . I turned it in—"

"That's how he knew you must be in trouble . . . that and Belmont's disappearance from the Paris scene. He had a few contacts in the same shady circles and found out that Tony had been boasting about a blackmail scheme. He put it all together, but Tony had a few weeks' start on him. He had to wait in jail for a little while for his hearing.

"Derek knew Belmont thought you had the money, but he knew better because the police had connected it to him and told him about it. They knew nothing about its source; he decided that discretion was the better part of valor and denied knowledge of it himself. It must have been painful for him." Jason chuckled.

"Poor Derek," Eleanor said. "But the twenty thousand faded from Tony's mind, too, you know. He was convinced that you had stolen the formula and were worth millions, Jason. That was what drove him. And . . . I'm sorry to say, he convinced me enough that when I saw the suicide note, I believed that Lorraine and you had both been involved."

Jason patted her reassuringly. "It was a pretty clever scheme of Paul's. Easy enough to fake the note, of course, just by typing it instead of writing it."

A guilty memory stole over Eleanor. "I know. I

wrote a new one, myself. Paul pretended it was beyond him to fake the signature, and I did that myself, too."

"But why?"

"I couldn't let the authorities see what Lorraine had written. it seemed to accuse you of things. . . ."

"Things you believed?" Jason's brows rose in wonder.

"It doesn't matter now, Jason. Please, let's just forget all about it. We can sort it out with Samir and Derek and the police. Right now all I want is for you to hold me and tell me everything's going to be all right. . . ."

And Jason did for a long, quiet time as the eastern sky steadily brightened and dawn became morning. Eleanor knew that she would never let anything come between them again.

THEY SPENT HOURS later in the day going over and over the details with Derek. Eventually all their questions were answered, and they could feel some sense of relief.

The entire camp was numb, both at Lorraine's death and at the revelations concerning Paul. The team, now sadly depleted, did not work that day.

Eleanor was able to share their subdued joy, however, when Jason made his announcement. The virus had been isolated, and even now a vaccine serum was being prepared for shipment to them. They could start testing the following week. If all went well, the Syrian government would institute a full vaccination program immediately. The long, grueling struggle was over.

Eleanor sat savoring this one positive development. Jason was talking excitedly with Myriam, Samir and Claude. They deserved this, Eleanor thought warmly, especially now that tragedy had torn their group apart.

Eleanor stayed in the background, watching them with a lump in her throat. Suddenly, very quietly, Derek was beside her. He looked shyly into her eyes, trying to read them.

"I'd like you to be proud of me like that someday," he said quietly.

Eleanor smiled through tears...the tears of relief and gratitude.

"At least you showed up this time," she teased. "Now maybe you'll take up some honest work."

"I've had a few shocks, too. A few weeks in jail...Tony's death. But the worst was when I realized what danger you were in. I knew then that it really had to end. But you'll see. It isn't only promises this time."

Eleanor gave him a quick hug. Jason came to her then. "I'll see what I can do when we get back to France. This young man could use a little guidance."

Derek grinned sheepishly.

"And now, my wife and I want to be alone," Jason said. He put his arm around her, and they went outside. They stood, facing the harsh desert landscape, and watched as hot breaths of wind sent whirls of sand scudding here and there. The sky was a shining arch of blue, almost unbearably intense.

"Do you know, I'm going to miss all this," Eleanor said.

"You'll be able to forget it once you're safely ensconced in your new home, deep in the green countryside of France—or won't you?" There was gentle mockery in Jason's voice.

"Oh, I don't know. I can't be sure, after all we've been through, whether I'll love or hate the memories of this desert."

"Do you know, I think I'll love *my* memories of being with you here, and then almost losing you, and then having you back—completely this time," said Jason. And he hushed anything further Eleanor might say with a long, deep kiss that poured his soul into hers. Lost in his warmth and the safety of his arms, Eleanor could think only of their future together. The long ordeal was over.

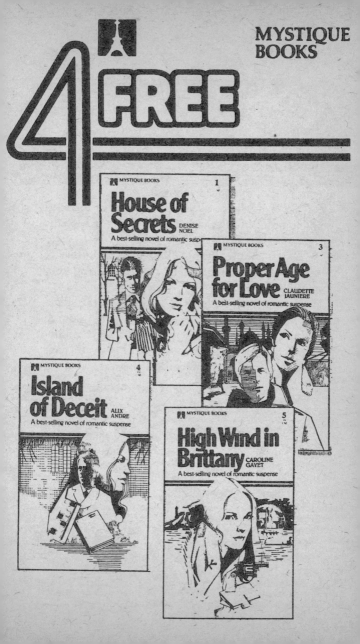

Everything you've always expected in a book!

Exciting novels of romance, suspense and drama, with intriguing characters and surprising plot twists, set against international backgrounds.

You will receive the newest in romantic suspense as soon as it's available!

As a Mystique subscriber you will automatically receive 4 new releases a month. Each novel is far more than you'd expect—even better than you could hope for. A whole new gallery of surprising characters in chilling and dramatic situations. A riveting entertainment experience   and for only $1.50 each.

House of Secrets by Denise Noël

As the prosecutor accused her of murder, Pascale remained silent. To defend herself demanded revealing a family secret that had been kept for eight long years. When she'd been hired by the wealthy Sévrier family she'd not expected terror and heartbreak   nor death!

Proper Age for Love by Claudette Jaunière

Anne didn't understand when her fiancé suggested she become his mistress, not his wife. She left him and steeled her heart against love forever. But her world was shattered years later by the sound of his voice. Fearing her heart might yet answer his call she fled .   into a nightmare!

Island of Deceit by Alix André

Despite a threat to her life, Rosalie had to learn what had happened to her sister on the exotic Caribbean island of Sainte-Victoire. She soon found herself enmeshed in a web of intrigue   and in love with the one man she had most reason to fear

High Wind in Brittany by Caroline Gayet

For weeks the tiny fishing village had been aflame with rumors about the mysterious stranger Why had he come? What was he after? When Marie learned the truth she could not hold back her tears She wept for him, for the townsfolk, but mostly   for herself

Your FREE gift includes

House of Secrets—by Denise Noël
Proper Age for Love—by Claudette Jaunière
Island of Deceit—by Alix André
High Wind in Brittany—by Caroline Gayet

Mail this coupon today!

FREE GIFT CERTIFICATE
and Subscription Reservation

Mail this coupon today.
To: Mystique Books

In U.S.A.
M.P.O. Box 707
Niagara Falls, NY 14302

In Canada
649 Ontario Street
Stratford, Ontario, M5A 6W2

Please send me my 4 Mystique Books **free.**
Also, reserve a subscription to the 4 NEW
Mystique Books published each month. Each
month I will receive 4 NEW Mystique Books at
the low price of $1.50 [total $6.00 a month].

There are no shipping and handling nor any
other hidden charges. I may cancel this
arrangement at any time, but even if I do, these
first 4 books are still mine to keep.

My present
membership
number is

NAME   (PLEASE PRINT)

ADDRESS

CITY   STATE/PROV.   ZIP/POSTAL CODE

Offer not valid for present Mystique subscribers.
Offer expires March 31, 1981
Prices subject to change without notice.

09096